The bell rings. The teacher gets up.

"Hello," she says. "My name is Miss Shumway. If I'm not mistaken this is Junior English, first period."

She's nervous. Very. Not a good sign. I would like this to work out for her because she's young and she's cute. She also gave me a smile when I first walked through the door. Which I ignored.

Miss Shumway reaches across her desk for a neat stack of papers. She knocks over a vase of flowers. Someone in the back laughs. Miss Shumway just stands there frozen like a statue. Then suddenly she grabs some paper towels from a drawer and starts to blot up the water. By the time she has everything all cleaned up, her face is bright red.

It would be best if she could make some joke or pretend she isn't bothered. She doesn't do either one. Instead she starts talking about class rules in a high rattly voice.

"This is what I expect," she says.

Just then someone walks through the door. It's the girl from Ken's Drive-In. The one with the legs. Marti to her friends. Martha to me.

"I expect," Miss Shumway says, her voice getting even higher, "people to be on time."

"I'm sorry," says Marti. She ducks her head a little and slips to the back of the room. She doesn't see me, but I get a good look at her. She's dressed all wrong— cords, running shoes, a T-shirt that says ONE NUCLEAR BOMB CAN RUIN YOUR WHOLE DAY.

In case you're interested, my heart is pounding.

A. E. CANNON lives with her husband and sons and their many pets in Salt Lake City.

ALSO AVAILABLE IN LAUREL-LEAF BOOKS:

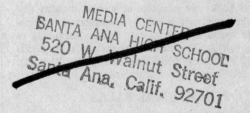

Cal Cameron by Day, Spider-Man™ by Night

PB

A. E. Cannon

LAUREL-LEAF
BOOKS

LAUREL-LEAF BOOKS bring together under a single imprint outstanding works of fiction and nonfiction particularly suitable for young adult readers, both in and out of the classroom. Charles F. Reasoner, Professor Emeritus of Children's Literature and Reading, New York University, is consultant to this series.

Published by
Dell Publishing
a division of
The Bantam Doubleday Dell Publishing Group, Inc.
666 Fifth Avenue
New York, New York 10103

ISBN: 0-440-20313-9

RL: 5.9

Reprinted by arrangement with Delacorte Press

Printed in the United States of America

April 1989

10 9 8 7 6 5 4 3 2 1

KRI

For Ken

Prologue

There's a crazy old guy who lives in our town named Quentin Q. Payne. Seriously. Mr. Payne is about sixty years old, and he spends his days wandering around town, smoking and mumbling to himself. You probably have at least one guy like this where you live too.

Some of the guys at school like to fool around with old Mr. Payne. They buy him coffee and get him to talk. Mr. Payne tells them all sorts of bizarre things, like he's directing a movie starring Jesus Christ, for instance.

I leave Mr. Payne pretty much alone. He scares me. That's right. Scares *me*, Calvin Cameron, high school quarterback and all-around hotshot. I look at him sprinkling cigarette ash all over himself and I wonder what he was like before he lost it. Did he like baseball? Girls? Mexican food? What kind of a guy was he? Or didn't he know? Maybe the guy never had time to find out.

And that's the thought that terrifies me.

1

Here I am at the mall with a couple of guys, playing video games, hustling chicks, giving salesclerks a bad time. I'm here with Sean Young and Mike Mangum. Sean is what I guess you'd call the Big Man on Campus. He calls all the shots. He always has, ever since grade school. When I was new at Washington Elementary (our old grade school), Sean used to beat me up and steal my lunch money. I still wanted him to be my friend, though, because he was the most popular guy in our class. I finally made him like me and we've been friends ever since. Mike Mangum is another long-time pal. He's big and blond and lopes around like a grizzly. Everyone calls him Bear.

Right now we're checking out a booth sitting in the middle of the mall. It has flashing lights and a sign that says

PLUMB THE HIDDEN DEPTHS OF YOUR OWN PERSONALITY:
COMPUTERIZED HANDWRITING ANALYSIS,
$1.00.

"Hey, what is this?" says Sean. A girl who is sitting in the booth sets down a book she was reading. She has glasses and bad skin, just the kind of girl who works in the school library one period a day.

"It's a handwriting analysis machine," she says, turning a little pink in the cheeks. Then she picks up her book again. It's called *Love's Sweet Surrender*.

Sean and Bear both howl and echo, "A handwriting

analysis machine!" The girl squirms a little and puts down her book. Her glasses slide to the end of her nose. For some reason, girls like her always get that way around guys like Sean and Bear. And I guess around guys like me. Jocks, I guess is what we're called at our school, although you really don't have to play sports to be a jock—you just have to dress right and shoot off your mouth.

Anyway, I sort of hate to see her get so bothered, so I joke around. "Well, I guess I'll plumb the depths," I say.

I reach into my pocket, pull out my wallet, and find a dollar. I hand it to the girl, who grabs it away from me like she's afraid I might change my mind.

"Here," she says, shoving a computer card and a pencil toward me. "Sign your name on the line there."

"Thanks," I say, and I make a move to smile, but she looks away. So finally I take the card and the pencil and I write out my full name: Calvin Simpson Cameron.

"There," I say, handing it back to her. The girl takes it and puts it into this little slot, and all the lights on the computer light up. The machine makes a whirring noise, and ten seconds later it spits out this piece of blue paper.

"Here," says the girl, picking it up from the bin where it dropped. "Here's your handwriting analysis." She puts it down on the counter and picks up her book again.

"Let's see what it says," says Bear.

I open it up and read in a high voice just like Mr. Farrell's, the drama teacher. "It says here that I am intelligent, sensitive, and basically decent, with a tendency to hide my real feelings."

Both Bear and Sean whistle and make kissing noises.

"Say, that's our Cal," says Sean. "Such a sweet boy."

I look upward and bat my eyelashes. The girl in the booth blushes again. Then she shifts her weight and turns her back on us.

"Hey," Sean bellows, "I want to do it too."

The girl turns back around.

"That'll be a dollar," she says through real tight lips.

"You know," says Sean, digging into his pocket, "you really ought to loosen up. Okay? Think you can do that for us?"

I hold my breath for a minute, hoping Sean will shut up, which he does when the girl hands him a pencil and punch card. He presses the pencil hard against the card.

"Okay," he says. "Here it is."

The girl takes it and feeds it into the machine. The lights flash and a blue piece of paper appears, just like before. Bear and I crowd around Sean when she hands it to him. The paper says "You are intelligent, sensitive, and basically decent, with a tendency to hide your real feelings."

"Wow!" says Bear. "Déjà vu!" He and I laugh. Not Sean.

"Hey," says Sean, sounding like a kid who has just had something taken away from him, "this one is just like yours, Cameron."

I shrug. "Guess we're just a couple of sweethearts," I say.

Sean turns to look at the girl.

"You know something," he says to her in a loud voice. "Your machine really stinks, you know that?"

She doesn't say anything, but her cheeks are bright pink.

"Hey, come off it," Bear says. "Let's go to 7-Eleven and play a couple of games."

So we leave the mall and walk down the street a couple of blocks to the 7-Eleven. As we cross the street, I take my handwriting analysis and crumple it up into a tiny ball, and when no one is looking, I throw it away.

When I get home I have a little surprise. My brother's car is parked in the driveway.

Good old Eugene. Eugene the Genius, Eugene the Computer Head.

Home for term break.

I let out a little sigh and pull up in front of the house because Eugene's car sits right in the middle of the driveway. Just like always. There's barely enough room for my mom's BMW. I have to park my dad's car (otherwise known as the nerdmobile) out front.

When I walk through the front door I find everybody (Mom, Dad, and Eugene the Genius) in the living room having an intelligent conversation. This kind of conversation frequently takes place when Eugene's around.

Eugene notices me. "Hi, Calvin," he says. Eugene is the only person in the world besides my old third-grade teacher who calls me Calvin. Everyone else calls me Cal. Not Eugene though. He doesn't believe in shortcuts of any kind.

"Hi," I say. I plop down in the leather armchair. I resist picking up the new *Sports Illustrated* sitting on the coffee table. I've heard it's impolite to read while people are talking to you.

"What have you been doing, Cal?" my dad asks. I hate it when he asks that question. It's like he wants me to account for all the prizes and scholarships I've just won in the last forty-five minutes. The fact is that I'm not very much like my brother. Every time Eugene walks out the front door, someone's there handing him a citation for academic distinction. Me, on the other hand—people act like they're real surprised when they find out I know how to read. What, they practically say, he can play football and *read too?* I may not be the world's greatest student, but I hate it when I get that reaction. I really do.

I shrug.

"Well," my dad says again, "what have you been doing?"

"Whatever."

"Now, that's what I like," says my mom, getting up and walking toward me. "An articulate answer."

She slips an arm around my neck just like a lady wrestler. "Geez, Mom," I say, "you're killing me." I notice she's just had her hair done. She lets go and smiles. My mom is actually pretty good-looking.

"So," I say, turning to Eugene the G. and not knowing exactly what else to say, "how's college these days?"

Eugene started college this summer in Salt Lake City about forty miles north of here. Anyway, Eugene just sort of sits there and beams for a minute. "The finest experience of my life, Calvin. It really is. They're letting me take a few upper-division chemistry classes, and I'm a lab assistant for Dr. Mineer."

I look at Eugene, and for just a second I want him to drop completely dead. I hate all his scholarships and his upper-division chemistry classes and how smart he looks, and I really hate how my dad sits on the edge of his seat holding his breath, waiting for Eugene's next word. I decide to ask Eugene the only question that ever throws him.

"So like what do you do for fun, Eugene?"

"Well," he says after thinking for a minute, "there's a planetarium downtown. Some friends and I go down there quite often on the weekends."

I shift my weight. "Gee, that sounds really interesting, Eugene," I say, finally picking up that *Sports Illustrated.*

I guess I better explain something about my brother Eugene. Eugene the G. has always been a sci-fi-nik. When we were little kids he used to pretend he was blasting me with a laser. Then he'd scream, "Beam me aboard, Scotty!" So I guess it doesn't surprise me that Eugene gets his kicks cruising a planetarium on Saturday nights. What I want to know is how I got somebody like him for a brother.

My dad, on the other hand, is real pleased that he got somebody like Eugene for a son. It's not hard to see why. Eugene the G. and my dad like all the same boring stuff— plain vanilla ice cream, science magazines, chess. They play chess all the time. They always have. When I was little I once asked Dad if I could play with them. I wanted to be on his team or something. My dad just said that chess was a game for two people. I never asked again.

"Tell me, Calvin," said Eugene, "have you thought any more about taking admission tests this spring? It's a very good idea to take them the spring of your junior year, I believe."

"Eugene," I say, flipping a page, "I'm just starting my junior year."

"Well, you really ought to start making plans, Calvin," he says.

"That's what I tell him," pipes up my dad, "but he doesn't listen to me."

I keep reading. I'd hate my dad to think I was actually listening.

"Well, you at least registered for honors classes, didn't you?" I'll say this for Eugene. He sure doesn't know how to take a hint.

"No," I say, starting to get angry. "I didn't."

"Calm down, Cal," my mom says. "Eugene is just interested in what you're doing."

"No, he isn't," I say, standing up slowly. "He's only interested in what I'm *not* doing."

The three of them just stare at me. Eugene's mouth is slightly open, and suddenly I feel like a total jerk. I throw the magazine down in the chair and leave the house.

I feel even dumber once I get outside. I mean I came home in the first place because I was hungry, which is not all that unusual, but now I can't go back inside. Not after throwing a magazine around and making a scene like I was on daytime TV or something. I had this girlfriend once who watched all the soaps, which meant that whenever I was over there in the afternoon I got to watch them too. They kill me. Especially those blow-dry guys. Talk about phony. But here I am, screaming at Eugene the G., who just blinks at me through those Coke-bottle glasses of his. I hate myself when I do stuff that makes me look stupid.

I remember it's Friday night, which means that the Geekman is probably working at Ken's Drive-In. He'll feed me. He won't like it and he'll tell me no at first, but he'll end up feeding me: large cherry Coke, lots of ice; a cheeseburger; and a large order of fries. I get in the car.

The Geekman's real name is Walter Geke, which is about the worst name in the world I can think of to stick on a kid. And it doesn't help that Geke looks like he does. I mean he's really short, with a chest that looks like a beer keg. He was also born with one leg a lot shorter than the other, so he has to wear these special shoes. The Geekman comes from a very strange family, too. He told me his mother buys everyone seven toothbrushes—one for each day of the week—so that no one has to use yesterday's wet toothbrush. His dad spray-paints flowers red, white, and blue for the Fourth of July. His brother Ned drives a van done in camouflage. You get the picture.

I think if I looked like Wally and had Geke for a last name, I'd just keep quiet and smile a lot. That way no one would notice me. Not the Geekman, though. He never shuts up. He's the kind of guy who can really get on your nerves. He does, too. Sometimes the guys on the team will get so fed up with Geke (who is the team manager) that they'll pick him up and dump him in the trash can. I always end up sticking around and dragging him out, which makes him think we're best friends. He tells me things he doesn't tell anyone else, too. He tells me, for instance, that he wants to host his own talk show one day, just like Johnny Carson. He plans to use "Daniel Divine" as a stage name.

I pull up in front of Ken's Drive-In and park the car. Through the glass door I can see the Geekman taking orders behind the counter. He's got this little white paper hat pushed forward and to one side of his head. It kills me the way the Geekman wears hats. I go in.

"Hiya, Geke old buddy," I say as soon as he sees me.

He squints his beady little brown eyes as I walk toward the counter.

"You got any money?" he says.

I act very offended. "That's a pretty lousy question, Geke. How do you think that makes me feel?"

"So you got any money?"

"Sure," I say. "I've got money."

He grunts, still looking at me. Then he picks up a pencil and a little white pad of paper.

"Okay, so what do you want?"

"The usual," I tell him.

"Cherry Coke on the rocks, large order of fries, and cheeseburger to go."

"Make that to stay," I say, "then see if you can go on a break."

The Geekman starts punching some buttons on the adding machine. "That's three forty-seven," he says, eyeing me.

"Put it on my tab," I say.

"You said you had money, Cal!" he explodes.

"I do," I say. "It's in the bank."

"You wanna know something, creep?" the Geekman says. "You're gonna get me in trouble one of these days." He rips off the paper and yells my order back to the cook.

"See you in a minute," I say.

I go to the back of Ken's and sit in a booth by a window. I won't sit in a booth unless it's by a window. I like to look outside and stare at anything that happens to come my way.

The Geekman lets me sit here for a half an hour or so before he shows up carrying a tray with my order and something for him, too. Fries smothered with mayonnaise.

"This is how West Germans eat them," he always says. The Geekman is like that. Just full of useless information.

"I hope you realize I pay for all this stuff," he says.

"Thank you," I say. "You're a real sweet guy."

We eat for a while without talking. Before long the Geekman has mayonnaise drooling down his chin.

"Look, Geke," I say. "Will you wipe your chin please?"

He picks up a napkin and dabs at himself, just like an old lady with a lace hankie.

"How'd you feel about football practice today?" says the Geekman finally.

I shrug. The truth is I didn't feel good about it at all. In fact, I've had a lousy week. I can't figure out what's wrong with me. Let me explain. Last year Sean, Bear, and I played on the varsity football team even though we were only sophomores. The three of us even got our pictures and a writeup in the local paper. The article called us "triple trouble." You're probably saying to yourself, "These guys were hot stuff." And you're right. And now everybody is expecting us to be wonderful this year.

But here I am, fumbling snaps and throwing interceptions in practice. My head is completely someplace else. The truth is, I don't feel like doing football right now. The truth is, I don't feel like doing anything right now. I tell myself I'll get motivated once school starts next week.

"Well, Opie," says Geke, "you looked a bit tuckered out this afternoon." Did I mention that the Geekman does TV characters? Like right now he's Andy Taylor from Mayberry. It's pretty obnoxious.

"Look, Geke, do you mind?" I say, "Let's not talk about football right now, okay?"

Actually, I've got other things on my mind. Like this girl who just walked through the door.

She's probably about five-seven, with hair to her shoulders so blond that it's practically white. She has a square face and small bright blue eyes. Hardly any makeup. And the strongest looking legs I've ever seen on a girl.

I need to explain something a little strange about myself here. When I was in the sixth grade, I had a crush on this girl in our class named Elsapeth who came from Austria. She couldn't say much at first, just something like "My name is Elsapeth, I come from Austria," but she could kick the skin off any kind of ball. Kickball was the big game at our school, and this girl Elsapeth could kick the ball farther than any guy in the class because she had real Charles Atlas *legs*, which I think she probably got from hiking around and yodeling in the Alps all day.

So the thing is this: I've always liked girls with legs that last, and I like the way this blond girl isn't trying to cover them up. Most girls I know with muscles like to make you think they don't have any.

"Who's that?" I say.

The Geekman cranes his neck around, which makes him look exactly like a gooney bird.

"Geke," I say, "will you stop it? Didn't your mother teach you not to stare?" Of course she didn't. Geke's mother probably stares too.

"Make up your mind, Cal. First you say 'Who's that?' so I try to help you out by looking, then you say 'Don't look.' Why don't you try a little consideration for a change?" The Geekman is practically yelling at me.

"Shut up, Geke."

The girl walks over to the counter, but she looks our way for a second. Maybe two seconds.

"Look, Geke, will you take off that stupid hat?"

"It's not a stupid hat. For your information, I wear it with pride. It's part of my uniform." He looks at his watch. "I gotta get back to work."

For once the Geekman's timing can be considered nothing short of terrific.

"Hey, Cal," he says, clearing up the trays, "I need a ride home. Can you come get me?"

"What time?" I ask, trying to look at the girl without her knowing.

"I usually get things all closed by two o'clock."

"In the morning, Geke? Come on." I shove my hands into my pockets. Then I say, "Okay. But don't mess around. I won't wait after two."

"Hey, thanks, Gomer!" Geke shouts. He gives me this stupid little salute he always gives when he says good-bye, and then he disappears behind a swinging door that says EMPLOYEES ONLY.

The girl finishes giving her order and walks over to the Ms. Pac-Man game in the corner of Ken's. She fumbles around in her pocket for a few quarters.

Most girls I know won't play video games. I can't ever remember going into a place and seeing a bunch of girls hanging around a game. Can you? I decide to go watch her.

She plunks in a quarter and then starts twisting the knob around. I keep waiting for the sound that says her Pac-Man croaked, but it doesn't come. She just keeps standing there twisting the knob. This girl is really good, I say to myself.

A couple more minutes go by and she's still standing there at the machine. Somebody calls over the counter, "Number sixty-three."

The girl leaves the machine, even though she still has playing time, and picks up her order. She sits down in a booth close to where I'm standing. I walk over.

"Hey, you're pretty good."

She smiles. Her mouth is closed because she's just taken a bite out of her burger.

I sit down in the booth across from her. I notice her T-shirt. There are pictures of heads and words that say,

Meet the Marx Brothers:
Groucho, Harpo, Chico, Zeppo and Karl.

"I like your T-shirt."

She wipes her mouth. "So you get it?"

I shrug. "Sure. I mean the Marx brothers. Everyone knows who they were. Pretty funny guys." I remember this guy in my biology class last year named Dash who did a pretty good Groucho Marx imitation while dissecting a fetal pig.

She stares at me, then shakes her head. She laughs.

I smile. "What's so funny?"

"Nothing." But she's still smiling to herself.

I don't know what to say, because all of a sudden I'm feeling stupid and I don't even know why.

"Anyway," she says, "I like T-shirts. I have a T-shirt collection. I just got one the other day. It says

Ladies Sewing Circle and Terrorist Society."

I just stare at her, thinking that she may be a little weird. She looks at me, her head tilted a little, and then she shrugs. "Oh, well. I thought it was funny." She picks up her hamburger and starts eating it again.

Of all the conversations I've had with girls, this one certainly isn't. I decide to go home. Before I leave, though, I try one more time.

"What's your name, anyway?"

She smiles at me, and I can't help but notice that she has perfect teeth, which probably comes from me being the son of a dentist.

"My friends call me Marti," she says, "so you can call me Martha."

"You know something," I say, "you're a real funny chick. Lots of laughs." I leave and I don't even answer the Geekman as he screams good-bye to me.

* * *

So I decide to go to the canyon, which is where I always go when I want to get away. The canyon isn't far from Ken's or anywhere else in Provo. I get on Canyon Road and drive north out of the city and in fifteen minutes I'm driving up the canyon. There's no one else on the road, so I go faster than I should. I'd probably go faster than I should even if there was someone else on the road. I turn up the radio real loud and I try to forget how *stupid* I'm feeling.

I hate feeling stupid. And I hate anybody that makes me feel stupid. Like my dad sometimes. I mean sometimes I feel like I really hate my dad. My dad's a funny guy. I have to say that I don't understand him most of the time. To look at him he seems like a pretty ordinary type of father. Medium height, medium build, a little paunchy, skinny arms, that color of gray-brown hair a million other guys his age have, glasses. And he dresses just like every other dentist I've ever met—sports shirts and double-knit slacks all the way. At least Mom finally convinced him to stop wearing his lime green leisure suit. Who knows though? Maybe he still has it tucked away in his closet somewhere so he can take it out and put it on when no one's around.

So here he is, this really average-looking guy, who you'd expect to be like an average father who wants his son to play football and hustle girls. Not my dad. All he cares about are grades, grades, grades. I think he'd love me to be secretary-treasurer of the Honor Society so I could come home and report on the minutes of all their meetings. All through junior high school he wanted to be in the quest classes, just like Eugene was. Old Eugene the Genius.

The point is that I didn't want to be in any of those classes. My favorite class when I was in junior high was the class I had to take after I flunked out of beginning band. It was called Life Skills and it was a class designed for potential juvenile delinquents. Did I say *potential*? It was for twelve-year-old boys who already were juvenile delinquents. I was the only kid in that class who hadn't committed arson. But I guess they figured any kid who pulled a D minus out of beginning band was capable of sticking up a 7-Eleven. So there I was in that class with all those guys and we'd sit and listen to parole officers and reformed drug addicts and two ex-cons who told us we'd all better straighten up or die. I learned more from them than I ever did in any of the quest classes. Seriously.

Now my dad's big thing is college. He's always bugging me about getting applications and taking admissions exams. He's never asked me if I even want to go.

No one has asked me if I want to go. Not Dad. Not Coach. Not Eugene. Not even Mom. Everyone just figures I want to go to some big-name school and play football and get a degree in business so when I graduate I can make a lot of money.

Maybe that *is* what I want. And maybe it isn't. Maybe I'll want to sit on a park bench with guys like Mr. Payne and feed pigeons all day. I don't know. I just don't know.

I go even faster. I try to stop feeling. The radio starts to crackle. The higher I go, the more it crackles. I can only catch a few of the words the DJ is saying: "So Kelly blank, blank, this is for blank from Steve in West Valley blank."

And all of a sudden it hits me. There were five faces on the girl's T-shirt—Groucho, Harpo, Chico, Zeppo, and Karl. Karl Marx. Get it? If you don't get it right away either, then you know what I mean when I say that I'm feeling pretty stupid.

2

This is what I think of the first day of school.

The first day of school is just a big fashion show. You put on your latest threads, then you go to school, where you check out everyone else's latest threads. Even the lunch ladies go out and buy themselves new hairnets for the first day. See and be seen—that's the name of the game.

The only person I ever knew who didn't care what he wore the first day of school was Eugene. Eugene would wear his pajamas to school if our mom wasn't on hand to remind him to get dressed. Of course Eugene didn't care what he wore, because he didn't care what the guys running the show at our school thought.

I guess I care too much.

The fact is, though, if you want to be accepted at our school, you have to look "right," no matter what that "right" is. A few years ago, for instance, "right" was "preppy." I mean you went to school with your *hair* buttoned down. The look has changed since then—it changes all the time. The thing is to stay up with the changes. It's death if you don't.

I have English first period. So do Bear and Sean. A couple of junior cheerleaders are in the class too. So far so good.

The teacher is new this year. Young too. I'd say she looks a little like Princess Diana. Same blond hair. Same blue eyes. This should thrill Sean's girlfriend, Joy the Student Body, who loves Princess Diana.

A new teacher is a major gamble. A new teacher can either be terrific or terrible.

The bell rings. The teacher gets up.

"Hello," she says. "My name is Miss Shumway. If I'm not mistaken this is Junior English, first period."

She's nervous. Very. Not a good sign. I would like this to work out for her because she's young and she's cute. She also gave me a smile when I first walked through the door. Which I ignored.

Miss Shumway reaches across her desk for a neat stack of papers. She knocks over a vase of flowers. Someone in the back laughs. Miss Shumway just stands there frozen like a statue. Then suddenly she grabs some paper towels from a drawer and starts to blot up the water. By the time she has everything all cleaned up, her face is bright red.

It would be best if she could make some joke or pretend she isn't bothered. She doesn't do either one. Instead she starts talking about class rules in a high rattly voice.

"This is what I expect," she says.

Just then someone walks through the door. It's the girl from Ken's Drive-In. The one with the legs. Marti to her friends. Martha to me.

"I expect," Miss Shumway says, her voice getting even higher, "people to be on time."

"I'm sorry," says Marti. She ducks her head a little and slips to the back of the room. She doesn't see me, but I get a good look at her. She's dressed all wrong—cords, running shoes, a T-shirt that says

ONE NUCLEAR BOMB CAN RUIN YOUR WHOLE DAY.

In case you're interested, my heart is pounding.

Miss Shumway goes on, discussing one boring rule after another. The girl next to me is writing the name of some boy over and over again across the top of her desk.

I can hear kids ripping paper out of notebooks, riffling through books.

After the rules comes a diagnostic test. Miss Shumway wants to diagnose us.

And then—finally—comes the bell.

Out in the hall, Sean swears. "Where'd they find her?" he wants to know.

The Bear crumples the rule sheet into a little ball and sends it flying down the hallway with a perfect arc into a wastebasket.

"See you guys at lunch," I say.

I go to my locker to change books. While I've got my head buried inside, I hear a voice behind me.

"Hi."

I try very hard not to bump my head. I turn around. Marti is standing there.

"Hi," she says again with a smile. "I think I know you."

I don't know what to say, so she does me a big favor and carries on the conversation without me.

"We met at Ken's Drive-In about a week ago."

"Right," I finally manage to say. "I remember." Do I ever remember.

"Anyway," she says, "I think I may have sounded rude. I didn't mean to—I never mean to—but sometimes my mouth just gets in my way." She smiles and I happen to notice again what perfect teeth she has. My father would be very impressed with this girl.

"Forget it," I say. "I haven't thought about it one way or another."

She's looking at me like she doesn't believe a word I'm saying. If you want to know the truth, this girl is making me very nervous.

"Well okay, then," she says. She shrugs. "Do you want to go to lunch with me? I'll buy."

I think of Sean. What would Sean say about someone like Marti?

"Listen, thanks, but I can't."

I sound exactly like ice. Talk about a person's mouth getting in his way. This is not the way I'd like things to go at all.

Marti gives me another strange look. Then she says, "Maybe another time."

"Sure," I say. "Another time."

Kids are slamming their lockers shut up and down the hall. It's almost time for second period to start.

"See you later, Cal," Marti says. Then she disappears into the crowd.

It's 3:20. Time for football practice. Our first game is Friday.

All around me lockers are clanging and guys are laughing and shouting and everyone's almost dressed. Except for me. I'm sitting here on a bench with a tube sock dangling from my hand. I think it's been dangling there for about five minutes.

Something is definitely wrong here.

"Hey, Cameron!" someone shouts. "Hurry up, man!"

The problem is this. Sometime between fifth and sixth periods today I realized that I'm tired of having my body flattened on the football field for two hours each afternoon. Like the thrill is gone.

All of a sudden, the Geekman is flapping around my face like a huge moth.

"What's the problem here?" he wants to know.

"You're blocking my view, Geke."

The Geekman looks at me, then he looks at my sock. I can tell from his expression that he's going to shift into his Ward Cleaver imitation any moment.

"Now, Beav," he says, "you know what the coach will say if you're late."

The Geekman loves old TV shows—*Mister Ed, Dick Van*

Dyke, Donna Reed, Father Knows Best. He even knows the theme songs from all of them.

"Geke," I say, "sometimes I think you live to irritate me."

He just smiles.

"Now, now," he says. Then, "You know, June," he says to no one in particular, "the Beav isn't acting like himself these days."

I put the sock on and the Geekman disappears, probably off to count towels.

I manage to make it outside in time, blinking in the sun. Even though everyone wears the new fall threads the first day of school, September along the Wasatch front is actually still quite hot. Hot and bright.

We drop down for warmups. I don't feel like doing it, but I force myself. Before long the sweat is trickling down the sides of my face. I'm very glad that I sweat this way. When Eugene the G. sweats—which isn't often—the perspiration hangs in a little ball off the end of his nose. As you can imagine, this makes him look even stupider than usual.

"Okay," shouts Coach. "On your feet."

I groan inside. I mean I always hate drills, but today I feel like I'm dragging myself through a bad dream.

"Hey, Cameron," shouts one of the assistants, "pick 'em up!"

We make it through drills and then separate into our squads. Just as we break into formation, I look into the stands and my blood runs cold.

Granddad has come to practice.

He sees me at the same time I see him and gives me a jerky nod. Then he cups his hands around his mouth and shouts, "That's the way, laddie!"

"Hey, Cameron!" someone yells. "The old man's back from vacation!"

About five of the guys break for a second and wave to

Granddad. Granddad makes a fist and then punches the air over his head—just like he's Rocky Balboa. Geez.

"Okay, okay! Back to work, you clowns!" yells Coach, but he looks at Granddad and touches the brim of his hat.

I need to explain about Granddad. Granddad is from Glasgow, Scotland, which—if you've ever been there—looks a little like war-torn Europe. Even though Granddad's been here for over forty years, he still talks with an accent and he says things different. Like "kirk" for church, for instance, and worse, "laddie." To Granddad, any male younger than him is a laddie. He even calls my dad laddie, which really breaks me up. Here's my dad, this middle-aged dentist with white legs and a bald spot, and Granddad calls him laddie. Of course he calls me laddie, too. Ever since I was a Little Leaguer, he's come to all my games and practices, sat in the front row, and given me his repertoire at the top of his lungs: "That's the way, laddie!" "Give it to them, laddie!" and the worst, "Drop their stockings, laddie!"

Once after one of my Little League games, I told Mom to make Granddad stay home. Mom just looked at me with straight blue eyes and said, "Make him stay home yourself." Well, I never did, of course, and he's been coming ever since.

Actually, the guys like Granddad. They treat him like he's their mascot or something. Fine. It's just that I never wanted a mascot for a grandfather.

It's only about 125 degrees in the shade by the time we quit. Everybody is pretty wiped out. We listen to Coach wrap things up, then wait for him to dismiss us, which he does. As everyone starts hauling back to the locker room, Coach says, "Cameron! In my office. Now."

I get a few quick stares but no one says anything.

I have to wait by Coach's door for a while. He finally comes walking down the hall with the Geekman. He's checking his clipboard and giving the Geekman orders.

They both see me at the same time. Geke's face changes and he looks like he feels sorry for me. Coach takes his pen and puts it behind his ear. He turns to the Geekman once more. "Check back with me on that, Wally."

Geke gives that two-finger salute of his, then disappears.

"Okay, Cameron," Coach says, "come on in here."

Coach's office, which is right off the locker room, looks and smells like a couple of old shower stalls someone decided to turn into an office. There's tile on the walls, tile on the floors, tile on the ceiling. You can tell someone—his wife maybe—has tried to give the place a facelift. There are plants in macramé holders and photographs all over his bulletin board, along with a couple of signs done in basic Crayola that say "We Love you, Daddy." Still, I've always thought Coach's office was one of the more depressing places I've visited. It's the kind of place that makes you want to spray your chair for fungus before you sit down.

"Sit down there, Cameron." Coach points to a chair. I sit.

Coach slides as slow as a bear into his swivel seat behind the desk.

My palms are getting sticky.

Coach engages me in a little eye-to-eye contact across his desktop. Finally he says, "Cal, I'm putting Dillon ahead of you Friday."

I wait for it to feel like someone has kicked me in the stomach. But it doesn't. Very calmly and politely I say, "Fine."

Coach just stares at me.

I feel like I ought to say something. I always feel that way when it gets silent. "If Dillon is better, then he ought to play in front of me, Coach. I understand that."

Coach snorts at this. "Well, then, you understand a damn sight more than I do. You're bigger, stronger, faster, and quicker than Dillon. The only thing he's got going for him is that he wants it more."

He looks at me again, and this time I look at the floor.

"What's the matter, Cameron? What's going on here?"

I just shrug and shake my head and don't say a word. I can't, because I don't know what to say.

There are still plenty of guys hanging around the locker room, including Tad Dillon, who looks at me quickly, then looks away. I figure part of him is worried about what I might think, although I can see from his eyes that this is probably the happiest day of his life. Even better than the day he first noticed hair on his chest, probably. Bear, his hair still wet and uncombed, comes over to my locker.

"So what happened?" he says in a low voice.

"No big deal," I say, taking off my jersey. "Coach says I'm not starting Friday."

Bear swears.

"Look," I say reasonably, "he's just doing what he thinks is best."

Bear stands around for a minute, letting the water run into his eyes. Finally he asks if I need a ride.

I shake my head. "Granddad will give me a ride. He never leaves without talking to me."

Bear says good-bye and I finish pulling my things together. Sure enough, I find Granddad waiting for me outside. The skin around his eyes crinkles, which is as close as he gets to smiling.

"Hey, Granddad."

Granddad looks at me, then pulls the brim of his cap forward a little. "You're late, laddie."

"Yeah, I know. Sorry, Granddad."

We walk out to the parking lot. I see the Ole Grey Goose there. Ole Grey Goose is the name of Granddad's camper and pickup. It's the closest thing he has to a girlfriend. He loves that truck.

We crawl into the cab together and drive home. I can't tell if it's that Granddad senses something is wrong, but he doesn't say anything. We finally pull up in front of the house. I grab my gear and get out.

"Want to come in, Granddad? I'll make you some tea."

"Naw. Not now." He puts the truck in first and revs the engine. "Your mother is having me over for dinner tonight."

"Okay, Granddad." I shut the door. "See you later, then."

Granddad sticks out his chin about a mile and nods. Then he leaves me standing alone.

At dinner we have the fresh trout that Granddad brought back from his trip. Everybody likes trout, except my dad, who's doing his best to take little bites and move things around on his plate a lot. He ought to know by now, though, that he can't fool Granddad.

"How's your fish, Sandy?" says Granddad, talking to my dad.

"Good. Thank you."

Granddad rivets Dad to the wall with a stare.

"Then why are you not eating it? You think I canna see what you're doing?"

My dad doesn't say anything, but from where I sit I can see the back of his neck go red. Finally he says, "I'm not hungry tonight."

Granddad makes the snorting noise he always makes when he thinks someone is lying.

"Oh, for Pete's sake, Pop!" my father says.

I'm looking at my plate. This scene between my grandfather and father is bothering me a lot, although I can't figure out why. Eugene is quiet, too. Finally my mom breaks in.

"Dad, I haven't heard anything about your trip yet." She's asking for it, of course. Once Granddad gets going he's hard to stifle. But for right now, at least, no one minds.

Later, after dinner, when Eugene and I are cleaning up the kitchen, Eugene says, "Granddad can be such a tyrannical old fart." I look at Eugene in surprise. He hardly ever uses words like that. Old fart, I mean. Not tyrannical.

"Well, you saw the way he was picking on Dad, didn't you? Like Dad was a little kid again."

I always take the opposite position on any given subject when I talk to Eugene. I have those kind of principles. "I thought you'd be glad that Granddad wasn't picking on you for a change." Picking on Eugene is one of Granddad's hobbies. And then I add, "Besides, Dad was acting like a little kid. Moving his fish around on the plate like that. Geez. I'm surprised he wasn't hiding it in his napkin."

I don't really mean anything by all this, so I'm surprised when Eugene practically hops down my throat.

"You are so incredibly antagonistic toward Dad, Calvin."

"Antagonistic?"

Eugene just looks at me. Then he finally says, "Stop playing stupid." He rinses off another plate and hands it to me to dry.

Later I pick up my biology book and move out front to do a little homework on the front lawn, because it's still light outside. Miss Tanner, the biology teacher, has broken an unwritten law among teachers at our school: thou shalt not assign homework on the first day of school. Miss Tanner is obviously one of these teachers who don't care what kids think about her.

It still feels like a summer night outside although it's getting dark earlier. Down the street, someone is playing a radio full blast.

All I can say is that I certainly feel very strange. I've

never been one to sit around much and think about the way I feel, but right this very minute I can't get away from the fact that I feel lousy. Part of it is a delayed reaction to Coach's little bombshell, I'm sure. Okay, so that's natural enough. But it's more than that, too, only I don't know what.

I flip open my book and scan for a minute. Whoever had it last year started out great. Everything in the first chapter is underlined in the kind of yellow marking pen Eugene used to use until he read that underlining is an inefficient learning aid. Nothing in the following chapters is marked.

"Hi!"

I look up, startled.

It's Marti. She's dressed in a pair of running shorts and shoes, which isn't all that unusual. Girls wear running shorts and shoes all the time. What is unusual, though, is that she's actually been running. She's also got a big black dog with her.

I smile.

"This is Boy," she says. Boy gets all excited when he hears his name.

I put down my book. I get up and walk over. "Hey, fella." He lets me scratch his ears. "What kind of dog is he?" I ask.

"Black Lab. I've had him for three years."

We just sort of stand there for a minute or two. Then Marti says, "Is this where you live?"

I nod. "You live close by?"

"Oh, about two miles or so from here."

"You can run two miles? Without stopping?"

Marti smiles at me. "Sure. Can't you? I mean Wally told me you play football, so I assume you have to run."

"Well, yeah. Naturally. But I mean, that's different."

She looks at me with that funny see-through-you stare of hers and shrugs. "I don't see why it should be."

We talk for a few minutes about teachers, schedules, stuff like that. We find out that we both have Miss Tanner for biology. I have her third period. Marti has her fifth.

"What do you think, her giving us homework like that the first night," I say.

"Homework the first night wasn't all that unusual at my old school."

I try another angle. "I wonder if what they say about her is true."

Marti looks interested. "What's that?"

"Oh, you know. The stuff they always say about old-maid teachers who live with other old-maid teachers. You know what I mean?"

I know exactly how someone like Joy the Student Body would respond to that. She'd crinkle up her nose and squeal and say "Oh, for gross!" But Marti takes me completely by surprise.

She narrows her eyes a little. Then she says, "People's personal lives are their own. Besides, there are a lot of reasons besides that that women don't get married. Some just don't want to, for one thing."

This I find very hard to believe. "Don't you want to get married?"

Marti looks at me sideways, then smiles. I feel my ears go red, but I laugh too because she looks so—what's the word I want?—so sly. "Not right now." She lets out a sigh of relief.

"I mean in the future sometime."

"Maybe. Maybe not." A smile again. This time one that's straight at me. "Well, look," she finally says. "I've got to get going. See you tomorrow at school."

"Yeah. See you." I wave at her as she takes off. "Hey, Marti!"

She stops and turns around.

"I want to apologize for being such a *creep* about lunch today." I want to say more but I can't.

"Never mind." She smiles and waves me off.

I watch her and Boy until I can't see them anymore. Then I pick up my biology book and go inside. My mom and dad are in the living room talking. I hear my dad say, "You'd think after forty years he'd know I hate fish."

3

It's Friday night.

The game starts in twenty minutes. We'll go out to the field in about ten minutes. Everyone has just finished suiting up.

Bear comes up to me and says in a voice that no one else hears, "You okay?"

"Yeah, I'm fine."

Actually I'm numb. Last year before the first game I was so up I practically flew to the field from the locker room. But this year I'm just numb.

"Look, I'm gonna let someone get through to Dillon tonight." Bear plays center, which means he does double duty—he not only snaps the ball to the quarterback, he also acts as one of his main bodyguards.

"Hey," I say, "that's not necessary. It might also be stupid."

I'll say this. A lot of the guys are certainly bent out of shape about Dillon playing instead of me.

In a way it's kind of flattering, but they're not using their heads. Dillon deserves to play. Dillon knows it. Coach knows it. I know it.

"Awright guys!" Coach says. "Let's go!"

We leave the locker room and head for the field. The lights are on and the stands are full. I wonder who's here. I wonder if Marti has come. I'm pretty certain Granddad is here, unless dying was on his list of things to do today. He usually shows up an hour before the game with his thermos and blanket so he can locate his lucky spot in the center section of the bleachers.

I never even bothered to mention to the old guy that I probably won't be playing. I'm not sure, but I believe this qualifies me as a world-class jerk. What do you think?

We win the toss and elect to receive the ball. Sean takes the kickoff in the end zone and breaks a couple of tackles to get to the thirty-five yard line. Not a bad run. A real good run, in fact, but I can tell Sean wanted more. The truth is that Sean is the toughest player in the region. No one works harder on the football field than Sean Young.

On the side, Dillon puts on his helmet and trots out onto the field. It's his first play as a starting varsity quarterback. He throws a nice easy little screen pass to another receiver, Craig Kennedy. Picture perfect.

I feel a little ache in the pit of my stomach. What is wrong with me? Why am I not out there? I should be out there.

Why do I feel like I'm in the boxing ring these days—with me as my own opponent?

Anyway, we end up losing the game. Dillon worked real hard—I have to give him that—but with a minute to go he threw an interception that was run back for a touchdown. Final score: us 10, them 14.

By the way, I didn't see a minute of playing time.

After the game, Jennifer, who is a JV cheerleader and Joy the Student Body's best friend, ran up and hugged me and told me what a great game I had. I don't know if she was doing the old stand-by-your-man routine or if she just didn't notice I was on the bench instead of the field. Jennifer can be pretty phony at times. Like she'll be very friendly to someone and then, as soon as they turn around, make fun of them. I have to say that that bugs me sometimes. It really does.

Still, I prefer her reaction to my granddad's.

I find Granddad waiting for me with Mom and Eugene

outside the locker room door. I look for my dad. He hasn't shown, naturally. You can bet if Eugene were playing in the band he'd be here. No problem.

Eugene shoots me a look of sympathy. He's sorry about the game, I think, but mostly he's sorry about the way I'm going to catch it from the old man.

My mom laughs a little nervously. "Well," she says, and then she says "well" again.

Granddad has got his eyebrows scrunched together so that he has one long unbroken line of gray bristles running across his forehead. This is a pretty certain sign that he's mad.

"Do you need a ride home, honey?" Mom asks. She keeps shooting little looks at Granddad, warning him to behave himself.

"You knew you wouldna be playing tonight?" Granddad asks me.

"Yes," I say. "I knew."

"And you didna have the courage to tell me?"

I nod my head.

Granddad makes this very loud snorting noise and says, "Stand up on your own two feet, Calvin, and be a man."

I look around to see if anyone has heard Granddad. As far as I can tell, no one has. Granddad spins around on his heels like a tin soldier and marches off to the Ole Grey Goose by himself.

My mom takes my arm as she watches Granddad go. "Don't mind your grandfather. You know how he is."

"Yeah," I say. "I know how he is."

"You need a ride home, Calvin?" Eugene asks. He's being so nice I almost like him.

"Thanks, but no thanks," I say. "Some of the guys and I are getting together at Ken's. Bear will give me a lift."

Eugene nods. "Okay. See you when you get home, then."

So here I am, sitting around at Ken's with Bear and a

couple of other guys from the team. Sean is out on a very heavy date tonight with Joy the S.B. Sean is my friend and everything, but I have to say that he's just about the most predictable guy I know. Like it just figures he would go for the head junior varsity cheerleader, doesn't it.

Of course who walks through the door this very moment but the Geekman himself.

I can tell by the way he's dressed he's not coming in to work.

"Oh, no," shouts Bear. "We're doomed! It's the mighty Geke."

But the Geekman doesn't even notice us. He booms past and goes into the back.

We stare at each other. This is getting harder to believe by the minute.

"Hey," says one of the guys, "do you smell what I smell?"

It's hard not to. The Geek has put out a few dozen clouds of aftershave.

"Old Spice," Bear says. Then he starts to whistle just like the commercial on TV.

Geke is wearing slacks and a sportcoat. In addition to this, he has also combed his hair. You'd almost think he was going on a date by the way he's dressed.

We all stare at each other. Can it be possible? The Geekman seeing a girl?

The Geekman stumps out of the back room again. He has a full paper bag with grease stains on the sides.

"He's taking french fries?" someone says.

"Someone ought to warn the girl: beware of Geeks bearing gifts."

Everybody laughs.

The Geekman sees us for the first time. He looks startled. Guilty.

"So what did you do, Geke? Rip off the fries?" someone asks.

"None of your beeswax," the Geek snaps. Then he turns red in the face. "*Obviously* I didn't steal them. Shift managers are entitled to fries—whenever we want them."

We all act very impressed.

Geke is getting ruffled. "I'll see you yo-yos later," he says. "Much."

Everybody hassles him until he walks out the door. Then we turn and look at each other. "Yo-yos?" Bear says. We all crack up.

"Geez. Can you imagine the Geekman with a girl?" one of the guys says.

"Who is it, Cal? Geke seems to think you're his special buddy. What did he tell you?"

Everybody turns to look at me like I've got answers. I shrug.

"Hey, I do not encourage the Geekman to share his personal life with me," I say finally.

"Aw, come on," says someone.

"Honest," I say, "I don't." And now here's the part where I turn into a creep. Since I can't tell them anything about Geke's girlfriend, I feel I ought to give them something else. They expect something. Do you know what I mean? So I tell them Geke's little secret—how he wants to call himself Daniel Divine and take over the Johnny Carson show, how he practices monologues in front of his mirror at home.

I make everyone laugh, which I knew I would. I also make myself pretty sick. I shouldn't tell this stuff about the Geekman. I mean I really shouldn't.

And that's the end of that. We start talking about other things—school, Sean and Joy, the game. And nobody mentions Dillon.

Well, this is the news as of today:

1. Dillon is still playing ahead of me, and
2. Wally Geke has a date to the homecoming dance.

Although I find this very hard to believe, the second piece of news actually interests me more than the first piece. It's like I said before—I'm not all that interested in Geke's personal life—I mean the girl is probably just a female version of Wally Geke—but he's been so secretive about the whole thing that you can't help but be curious.

What can I say?

As for the first thing—Dillon is no great athlete, and that's the truth. But he's doing better than I would right now, and that also happens to be the truth.

We lost our last game, and some of the guys are pretty mad that Coach didn't pull Dillon and put me in. Frankly, I don't think I would have helped much. But people are getting upset. Upset with Coach. Upset with Dillon. Who they should really yell at is me. The truth is, I've thought about quitting the team—cleaning out my locker and splitting. In fact, I don't know why I don't.

Did I mention already that I think I'm going crazy? This is what I mean: on the outside I keep doing the same things I've always done—go to class, cut up, go to lunch, hang around the commons area with the guys, and talk to chicks, go to class, cut up some more, go to practice. But on the inside everything feels different. At times I feel like I'm watching myself as though I were somebody else in a movie or on TV. It's really weird.

Like right now, for instance. It's English class. In just three weeks the class has gone from bad to disaster. There's no way Miss Shumway can save it now, even though each Monday she starts out with a new set of rules and another lecture about classroom behavior. Sean and Bear are running the class now. And I guess I am, too.

Miss Shumway stands in front of the room. She looks tired, like she hasn't been to bed for a while. And her clothes don't look too good. I mean they're a little wrinkled—nothing too bad—but that really affects kids the wrong way. One of the history teachers here, for instance, wears little bits of everything he ate for lunch on his tie. It's pretty disgusting.

Anyway, Miss Shumway asks for yesterday's assignment. Sean raises his hand.

"Excuse me, Miss Shumway, but you said that was due tomorrow. I don't have it done and neither does anybody else."

Miss Shumway turns red. I can see that she's shaking. "I said the assignment would be due *today*."

Sean raises his hand again. She ignores him, but he speaks out anyway. "Excuse me, Miss Shumway, but you said that it was due tomorrow." Sean turns around and looks at the class. "Didn't she say that?"

Bear joins in, "That's what she said." He opens his folder. "See? I don't have it either. I think you should give us some time in class today."

No!" Miss Shumway is really upset. "Now, I told you the assignment was due today, didn't I?"

No one says anything. Then I hear a very matter-of-fact voice in the back of the room.

"The assignment was due today."

It's Marti.

Miss Shumway lets out her breath, like she's been holding it. Then she asks everyone to pass in their assignments. Everyone—except Sean and a few other guys, including me—pass their papers forward. I see that Sean is staring at Marti. I've seen that look before, too. He's trying to reduce her, to make her feel lower than a really thin layer of dirt. She doesn't even notice him. I mean she's not pretending to ignore him. She doesn't even seem to know he's in the same room. I wonder if Sean has ever had this experience before.

After class Sean says, "Who was that chick?"

Suddenly my stomach feels very nervous but I play it cool on the outside. "Her name's Marti something. She's new." I hope this will explain things some to Sean. What I hope is that he will just leave her alone.

Although I can't think of one good reason why I should care.

This is going to sound really weird, but I hang around the front lawn pulling weeds all evening long waiting for Marti and Boy to run by. I figure she probably will. I've seen her a few times since that first night we talked. She pretty much follows the same route at the same time every night. She's a really terrific runner—great stride and fast, too.

About 7:30 I see her and Boy start up the street. I position myself so that it doesn't look like I'm waiting for her, but so that she can't miss me either.

She gets closer.

She sees me and waves. Boy gives a big bark.

I drop a pile of dandelions and wave back. "Hi!"

She stops when she gets to the house and bends over, catching her breath. She is really sweating.

"Whew! I am beat tonight."

"I thought you looked pretty good," I say.

She raises her head and smiles. Her cheeks are bright red.

"Thanks."

I think of something to say. "Do you run track?"

She's stretching her calves out now. "No."

I really find this startling news. "Honest? You ought to."

She shrugs. "I'm not interested in being on any kind of team."

"Oh."

She looks at me, then laughs. "There I go again. You're on the football team, aren't you?"

I nod.

"I think that's great if that's what you want to do. I just don't see myself as a team kind of person."

That much is obvious, I think to myself, but I don't say anything.

"So how's school going for you, being new and everything?" I finally ask.

"It's okay," she said. "It really is. I didn't know what to expect when we moved here"—she shrugs—"but the classes are all right and I like some of my teachers really well. It's just too bad English class is such a mess. Usually that's one of my favorite subjects."

This is like the cue I've been waiting for.

"Yeah, can you believe it? What do you bet Miss Shumway doesn't last the year. I mean that lady is headed for a nervous breakdown."

Marti looks at me straight, really for the first time tonight since we've been talking. "Who are those guys? The ones that sit in the back and give her such a rotten time."

"Who? You mean Sean and Bear?"

"Yeah, those guys."

I get all ready to explain who they are and why she maybe shouldn't say much in class for a while when Marti says, "I know all about guys like that."

I'm getting all ready to defend Sean and Bear (especially Bear) when I notice Marti's face. She's angry. I mean *really* angry.

This makes me wonder. You're a strange girl, Ms. Martha, I say to myself.

Just then my dad pulls up in the nerdmobile. He gets out of the car and notices I am with a person of the opposite sex. Time for him to come over and say hello. He gets a big smile on his face.

"Hello, there, son," he says. "Out pulling weeds I see." Then he chuckles, like he's cracked a big joke. He's always doing that in social situations—saying something really ordinary, then laughing about it. At least, though, he doesn't ruffle my hair like he sometimes does. I just hate it when anyone touches my hair.

"Yeah. Dad, this is Martha Jeffs."

Marti flashes a terrific smile and I can see that my father is impressed. Dazzled even. It's obvious he hasn't seen a set of teeth this good all day long. I hold my breath and pray he doesn't say what I think he's going to say.

"You certainly have nice teeth, Martha."

Can you believe it? Most people say, "That's certainly a nice blouse you're wearing." But my dad hands out compliments on people's teeth.

Marti pretends my father has said something normal. "Thanks," she says, and smiles again. Dad says a couple more things, trying for a last look at her gums, then he goes into the house.

"What a nice guy," says Marti.

"Yeah, I guess," I say. "He's a little nuts about teeth. He's a dentist."

Marti laughs—a nice deep laugh. Then she says, "Well, Boy is getting ready to leave me, so I better go. See you tomorrow."

She takes off.

"Hey, wait a minute," I say.

Marti turns.

"You want to do anything Saturday?"

Did I just say that?

"Sure," she yells back at me. "Why don't you come with us first thing Saturday morning."

"What? And miss *The Amazing Spider-Man*?" *Spider-Man* is only the world's best cartoon.

Marti laughs. "You like *Spider-Man*?"

"Sure," I say, "but I'll miss him this week."

She waves and I sit there on the front lawn until she and Boy become two specks in the distance. Then I wonder who "us" is.

4

So I pick Marti up at seven o'clock in the morning. Saturday morning, if you can believe it.

"Do you mind telling me where we're going so early in the morning?" I say with a yawn.

"Birdwatching. Sort of," says Marti.

I practically slam on the brakes. "Birdwatching? You gotta be kidding."

Me, Cal Cameron, a birdwatcher? Sorry, but I can't see myself decked out with binoculars and field guides, if you want to know the truth. I tell Marti this and she laughs.

"Well," she says, "I guess we're not exactly going birdwatching. Miss Tanner says she knows a falconer . . ."

"A what?" I say.

"A falconer. You know, someone who keeps and trains falcons," Marti says.

"Oh, right," I say. Some people certainly have very strange hobbies. My granddad dated a lady who collected Frank Sinatra memorabilia. Then she died and her sister sang "My Way" at her funeral.

"Anyway," Marti goes on, "he's going to catch a hawk today—just pull it down from the sky—and Miss Tanner thought I'd be interested."

"Pull it down from the sky?" I say. This sounds very weird. "Come on."

Marti shrugs. "That's what Miss Tanner told me."

We drive to the school and pull into the faculty parking lot to the south of the biology room. Miss Tanner is already there with a kid I recognize from my biology class. Together they are loading things into Miss Tanner's van.

I have to mention something about this kid. Even though we have a class together, I don't know his name. He's one of those real shy guys who sits in the back of the classroom wearing a greasy Levi's jacket and bangs that are too long, never saying anything. You almost get to thinking that maybe God forgot to give him a personality.

When Miss Tanner sees us getting out of the nerdmobile, she waves.

"Cal, Marti, how are you? Danny and I are about ready to leave."

Danny. So that's his name. He nods at us both, and then he starts putting more things into the van.

"Okay," he says finally. "That's it."

We pile into the van together. Miss Tanner pulls out of the parking lot and heads for the canyon.

I find out we're going to a place not far from Cascade Springs. Danny explains that he's going to trap a hawk.

"Is it hard to do?" Marti asks.

Danny shrugs. "Not really—if you've got the right equipment and if you're patient."

It sounds pretty impossible, if you ask me. But this guy seems to think he's an expert, so who am I to say? Marti is acting like she thinks he's nothing short of wonderful. I personally notice that he has bad teeth.

We stop in a little mountain meadow—a clearing surrounded by trees.

"Here," says Danny. "We'll try it here."

He pulls a bunch of stuff out of the van and begins setting up on the meadow's edge. You can tell the trap is homemade—it's made out of stuff like yardsticks and badminton netting and string.

"Marti," Danny says, "can you get me the little white box inside the van?"

Marti jumps and disappears. She comes back with a tiny

white box. Danny opens it and takes out—get this—a mouse. I'll tell you the truth—seeing that mouse makes me a little sick to my stomach. Looking at my face, though, you can't tell how I feel. I've had a lot of practice telling my face what to do.

Danny takes the mouse and tethers it to the inside of the trap. It jumps around for a while, but it can't go anywhere, so it quiets down and sits real still.

"Come on," says Danny. Danny, Marti, Miss Tanner, and I leave the trap and move into the trees at the edge of the meadow. From where he sits, Danny can pull a string attached to the trap.

Whenever I go fishing with my granddad, he has a royal Scottish cow if I talk to him, so I keep my mouth shut. I don't know if catching birds is anything like catching fish, but I stay quiet just in case. I don't want a guy like Danny telling me to shut up in front of Marti.

And so we wait. And wait. And wait.

Marti whistles softly. Danny and Miss Tanner keep trading a pair of binoculars between them.

I, for one, begin to think we have wasted a perfectly fine Saturday morning.

Then Miss Tanner says, "There, Danny. Look."

He looks up and so do I. There's something in the sky overhead. It looks like it's standing still in the air. And then all of a sudden it falls onto the mouse like a rock out of the sky. Danny snags the string. The net collapses and a loud screeching fills the air.

"He got one!" screams Marti. "Danny caught a hawk."

Danny scrambles out to the net. The rest of us follow. Danny reaches into the netting and grabs the bird carefully with a gloved hand.

"A kestrel," he says.

It has eyes like an owl and a beak like an eagle. And it's screaming mad at Danny.

With his free hand, Danny pulls an old sock out of his

back pocket. He keeps talking to the bird in a nice calm voice. "There, girl," he says, "everything's okay. Nobody's going to hurt you."

Danny dangles the sock from his hand. I notice that it has a tiny hole cut in the toe with a leather thong threaded around it for a drawstring. With one swift move, Danny slides the bird into the sock headfirst. The kestrel pokes her head through the hole in the toe and screeches some more.

"That'll keep you safe and sound for a minute," Danny says. "She can see now," he tells us, "but she can't squeeze her shoulders through the hole."

"She's so small," Marti says. "Is she really a hawk?"

Danny smiles a little. "Well, if you want to be technical, a kestrel is really a falcon." And then he explains the difference between falcons and hawks. "But yes, a kestrel is a bird of prey—just like a peregrine or a red-tail hawk."

"Tell Marti and Cal what you're going to do with her," Miss Tanner says.

"Well," says Danny, looking at the kestrel again, "I'll be teaching her to fly free, then come back to me when I call."

"How long will that take?" asks Marti.

"Oh, a while. But I'll have her flying to the lure in a week," Danny says.

He isn't exactly bragging when he says this, but you can tell he's proud of what he does.

You may have noticed that I haven't said much. The fact is that as soon as I saw that bird stop dead overhead and then drop like a bullet on the mouse, I was completely blown away. I have never seen anything so incredible in my whole life. And to think this guy—this guy who's a total nobody at school—knew how to do it.

You may not believe me when I tell you this, but for a minute I am jealous. For a minute I wish I were Danny.

On the way down the canyon I don't say much. And I

don't say much to Marti either when I take her home. I'm thinking things through. I guess I can't talk and think at the same time. Unlike Eugene, I haven't had tons of practice in that area.

This is what I'm thinking. I'm thinking that Danny Petersen is the kind of kid you usually feel a little sorry for. You look at him slouching in his desk at the back of the classroom and you say to yourself, "Now here's one guy who will never be senior class president. Then you discover he has this other life, this secret life away from school that's actually a lot more interesting than most things you do. And suddenly you realize that a guy like Danny Petersen doesn't need to win an election or date Joy the Student Body or be your personal buddy to like himself.

I'm still thinking about this when I park the nerdmobile in the driveway and walk in through the back door. Granddad's there. So's my dad. Dad's face is several different shades of red. This is generally a pretty good sign that he's annoyed.

"Where have you been?" he explodes.

I go to the fridge and take out a carton of milk.

"Birdwatching," I say. As you can see, I'm still pretty much in a daze.

Granddad lets out with this horrible cackle of his. "Tee hee, tee hee!" he says. "Birdwatching! That's a good one, laddie."

My dad comes uncorked, especially when he sees me take a drink of milk straight from the carton.

"Did you ask me if you could take the car?" he asks.

"I guess not." I wipe my mouth with the back of my hand. Call me fussy, but I make it a point never to appear in public with milk moustaches.

"Cal," my dad says, "your mother needed the car this morning. You'll recall that hers is in the shop. But it was gone and so were you. We had to call your grandfather and borrow the truck."

I do something stupid. I laugh. I'm not laughing at my father—I'm laughing at the idea of Mom driving the Ole Grey Goose. A BMW it ain't.

But naturally, my father thinks I'm laughing at him. He looks at me. He looks at Granddad. Then he leaves the kitchen. I watch him go, and I wonder for the millionth time why he and I just don't seem to connect. Ever.

"Tee hee, laddie," Granddad says. "Birdwatching."

5

"Wally's got a gir-r-r-rlfriend! Wally's got a gir-r-r-rlfriend!" Bear is dancing around the locker room, flipping Geke with a wet towel.

The Geekman is not taking this well. He needs to lighten up. Instead, he's stumping around like a very small bull, threatening Bear with towel demerits.

Tonight's the homecoming dance.

So far things are actually going all right. We won the game this afternoon. Dillon started but threw three interceptions in the first half, so Coach sent me in instead. I wasn't brilliant. But in the last minute of the game I connected with Sean in the end zone for the winning TD. High drama, as you can see.

Also, Jennifer is going with me to the dance. She's been a little frosty toward me the last few weeks, but she said yes, she would love to go with me to the dance. Very big of her, don't you think? And then tonight after the game, she practically knocked me over with a flying hug. "Oh Cal, oh Cal, oh Cal," she said. "You were wonderful."

So all in all, things are okay.

The Geekman is really making threats now.

"Hey, Bear," I say. "Lay off."

Bear makes one more loud snap with his towel, then joins me on the bench.

"Hey, swell game, buddy!" He shouts. Bear is in a really terrific mood. Everybody is. No one seems to notice Dillon standing by his locker alone. He's already showered and dressed and ready to split. He looks like he's going to go home and cry for a while before picking up his date. This is weird, but I kind of feel for the guy. Stupid, right?

I pick up Jennifer early. We're going to meet Sean and Bear and their dates at the nicest restaurant in Provo. I'll give you a hint. It isn't Ken's Drive-In.

Jennifer's mom, Mrs. Clark, opens the door. "Well hello, Calvin! Don't you look handsome! Come on in and sit down. Jennifer will be with you in just a minute."

I follow Mrs. Clark into the living room, where the whole family is sitting around watching TV.

"Say hi to Calvin, everybody."

Everyone mumbles a hello. Mr. Clark gets up to shake my hand. Then he settles down again to watch another swell episode of *Wheel of Fortune*.

The television is always on at the Clark house. Always. And it's always real loud. Plus you can usually find at least two or three of the Clark kids glued to the set. If anybody wants to say anything they have to yell. I don't know. Sometimes I come away from the Clark house feeling a little depressed.

I move some old newspapers and Legos from the couch so I can sit down.

"Oh, Vanna!" the TV set blares. Applause follows.

"Omigosh," says Jennifer's little sister. "Look at Vanna's dress. It's so-o-o-o gorgeous!"

"So, Calvin," shouts Mrs. Clark, "how's your football going?"

"Oh, okay, I guess." I shrug and smile.

"That's good." Mrs. Clark smiles.

Just about then Jennifer sweeps into the room. "Hi!"

"Hi yourself," I say. Jennifer looks major terrific tonight and she knows it. "You look great," I tell her.

Mrs. Clark slips an arm around Jennifer's neck. "Now be a good girl tonight," she says.

"Right, Mom." Jennifer gives me a wink.

"We'll see you two kids later." Mrs. Clark follows us to the door and waves.

We get into the car and start for the restaurant. Jennifer sits so close she's practically in my lap. I'm having a little difficulty concentrating on road signs at the moment.

We show up at the restaurant twenty minutes late. Sean and Bear are already there. They've given their names to the hostess and are waiting to be seated.

" 'Bout time, guys," Sean says.

"Couldn't tear ourselves away from *Wheel of Fortune*," I say. Jennifer shoots me a very dirty look. Stupid for me to say. But for some reason I'm feeling a little bugged tonight. I never noticed before how much Jennifer's family depresses me.

"Hey!" Sean gets the hostess's attention. "We're all here now."

"All right," she says. "If you'll follow me please."

The hostess is an old woman. Old enough to be someone's grandmother even. She's wearing a really stupid white blouse and a green skirt that goes all the way to the floor. It's her costume, I guess. They probably make her wear it. They probably say, "You can't work here unless you wear this stupid outfit." For just a minute I feel really sorry for her, being her age and having to stand up on her feet taking people to their tables all night. What a lousy way to spend the twilight years.

"I wonder what dinosaur dig they found her in," Sean says after we're all seated. Everyone laughs but me. Well, that's not exactly true: I do laugh—a little. There's no point in looking weird.

We've been at our seats for a while, eating appetizers and shooting the bull about football and school, when the most amazing thing happens.

Who should show up but Wally Geke with his date.

"Hey. Take a look at this," says Bear.

I turn around and look.

"Who's the girl?" says Joy.

The girl is Marti.

"I know her," Sean says. "That's the girl in our English class!" His eyes get a little squinty. "Remember her?"

"Yeah, right," says Bear. Then he mimics Marti. "The assignment was due today."

I have to tell you this right now. Marti looks like dynamite, in spite of the fact that her escort is Wally Geke. No T-shirt tonight. Instead, she's wearing a really simple white dress made out of slippery looking material. Not gobs of makeup. Straight clean hair. The only thing wrong with this picture is her corsage. It's got Wally Geke written all over it. Huge and purple and orange, it's the kind of flower you might want to give your girlfriend if your girlfriend is an extraterrestrial.

They follow the hostess into the next room.

"Well, you gotta feel sorry for a girl who goes out with Wally Geke," Melissa says finally. And with that, everyone turns back to the relish tray.

Well, well, well. The Geekman sure pulled a fast one on all of us. He has a date, and his date is Marti. I can only half hear what everyone is saying because my ears are pounding. This also means they're probably turning red. Eugene used to tease me about my ears when we were little. He'd ask me if I could make my belly button turn red, too. Then I got bigger than him so he stopped bothering me.

"For sure Miss Shumway is having a nervous breakdown," I hear Joy the S.B. say. "You can tell just by looking at her. I promise."

"How can you tell?" asks Sean.

"I can tell," says Joy, snapping a carrot in two with her teeth. "I watch Donahue in the summer."

I wonder what Marti and the Geekman are talking about.

"Oh, for awful," says Jennifer. Jennifer is always saying something like that. Oh, for gross. Oh, for rude. Oh, for disgusting. Oh, for darling. Oh, for you fill in the blank. Only when she says it it sounds like Oofer. Oofer gross. Oofer rude. Oofer disgusting. You get the idea.

"You don't think she'll do something weird in front of us, do you?" says Jennifer.

I hear Geke laugh in the next room. I know it's Geke, because he sounds a little like a donkey when he laughs. Actually, he sounds a lot like a donkey. It's pretty unforgettable.

I can't believe this. Marti says yes to a guy like the Geekman. And where did the Geek ever get the nerve to ask her in the first place?

Well, it looks like Marti has pretty well shot her chances of being anybody at Scenic View High. Of course, being Marti, she wouldn't care much anyway.

The next day I actually call Geke's house.

"Is Wally there?" I ask his mother.

"No," she says. "Walter is at work."

So I get in the nerdmobile and drive to Ken's.

When I check inside, I see Wally behind the counter, overseeing operations. It's very easy to make fun of Geke, but he actually does a good job. Like Eugene says, shift manager is the ideal job for power-hungry teenagers. It wouldn't surprise me if one day Geke becomes the Napoleon of fast foods.

I decide to surprise the Geekman. I stand in line to order and when I do, I actually pay. When they call my number, I take my tray to the corner booth. I'm probably there four or five minutes before Geke even notices me.

He makes arrangements, then he comes over to the booth.

"Where'd you get that food?" he asks.

"Burger King," I say, "but I prefer the atmosphere here. Come on. Where do you think I got it, Geke?"

He narrows his eyes. "How'd you get it?" he says finally.

"Well, Geke," I say, "you're never going to believe this, but I bought and paid for it myself."

I see that the Geek is really surprised. Stunned even. I laugh. "When do you go on break?"

"An hour from now."

I don't think I can stretch the onion rings for an hour. "I'll be back," I say.

When I come back later, he checks his apron. "Let's go," he says.

We get outside before I realize Geke is still wearing his shift manager's cap. Great. We look like we're going trick-or-treating.

It's really fall now. There are faded yellow leaves on the grass, the sidewalk, the gutter, just like scraps of old paper. I wish I'd worn a jacket.

"I saw you at the dance last night, Geke," I say finally.

"Well, excuse me." he says. Then he adds a little defensively, "I told you I was going." The Geekman stuffs his fists in his coat pockets.

"Yeah, you did."

We don't say anything.

"So did you have a nice time?" I ask.

"Did you have a nice time?" he mimics me. Then he says, "Yes, I did have a nice time, if you must know. Marti is a nice person. We laugh at all the same things."

Namely Geke's jokes, I imagine.

"So, are you guys serious? Two little lovebirds sitting in a tree?"

The Geek stops dead in his tracks. He looks at me. Then he says, "Knock it off, Calvin."

He's angry and I feel like a major jerk.

"Hey, I'm sorry," I say. "I was out of line."

Geke keeps staring straight ahead. He says very quietly, "I'm hardly the kind of guy that someone as terrific as Marti would be interested in."

I don't know what to say. I mean the Geekman no longer sounds like the Geekman. Usually he's busy telling you what an above average human being he is.

"Anyway, if you have to know," the Geekman continues, "I spent a lot of time talking about you—your times, how much you can bench press, stuff like that."

This embarrasses me so much I don't know what to do. Imagine some guy sitting there bragging to a girl about another guy's stats.

"Scratch that," Geke says. "I told her about your stats from *last* year. You ain't much to talk about these days."

"Touché, Geke."

The Geekman looks at his watch. "Well, I've got to be going back."

We turn around and start heading back up Ninth East.

In spite of myself, I'm dying of curiosity. "So what did Marti say?"

"About what?"

"Well, about me when you were talking about me."

"She said she thought maybe you were different."

"Oh." What a great thing to have a girl say about you.

"She meant it as a compliment. She likes different."

Obviously, I say to myself as I take a look at Geke in his stupid hat.

We walk in silence until we get back to Ken's.

As Wally turns to go in the door, I do something that surprises even myself.

"Hey, Geke," I say.

The Geekman turns to look at me.

"You're wrong."

"I am not. Wrong about what?"

"About your not being the kind of guy that terrific girls like."

He doesn't say anything. He just stands there. Then he salutes and disappears inside the building.

Oh, no, I tell myself. You may have just created a monster.

6

So this is what I do as soon as I get home. I make a phone call. This time I call Marti's house.

The phone rings. Marti answers.

"Hello?"

"Hello, Marti. This is Cal Cameron."

"Oh. Hi." She sounds happy enough to hear my voice. So far, so good.

"Listen, Marti," I say. "Have you gone running yet today?"

"As a matter of fact, no," she says. "I was just getting ready to go."

"How about if we go together? I'll drive us to Canyon Glen and then we can run up to Bridal Veil Falls and back."

"All right! That sounds great. What about Boy? Can he come, too?"

"Absolutely," I say. "Boy can come, too."

I pick Marti up. By the time we hit the canyon and park the car, I think I am nothing short of a genius. It's a perfect day for the hills. Cool but not cold. The sun high and bright. The leaves an M & M bagful of greens and oranges and yellows with some reds splashed around here and there. Marti is loving it.

"This is gorgeous," she says as we pump along together uphill. "I like the way that you have seasons here. We have seasons in San Leandro, too, but not like this."

"I never thought about it much, because I've always

lived here. But yeah, I guess I do too." Then I proceed to explain to Marti all about skiing in the winter and where everyone around here goes.

"What about cross-country skiing?" she asks. "I've always thought I'd like to give that a try someday."

Typical Marti, of course. Everybody around here downhills if they can afford it. It's the thing. You get all the right equipment. You buy all the right clothes. You go to all the right resorts. You make all the right moves, which means you parallel instead of snowplow. You don't talk about cross-country skiing. I mean you just don't.

But as a matter of fact, I do cross-country ski. When Eugene and I were little, our grandfather took us. I kept going even though Eugene moved on to better and bigger things like Junior Starters Chemistry Sets.

"Yeah. Well, I'll take you sometime, okay?"

Boy barks. Marti laughs.

We run along in silence for a while. Normally when things get quiet when I'm with a girl, I start to sweat. Not this time, though. I mean, for one thing, I'm already sweating, right? Besides, I just feel kind of comfortable. Like I don't have to talk all the time.

"You know," I say after a while, "I really don't know all that much about you." So I start to ask questions and Marti gives me her personal dossier:

—born in San Francisco.

—has one brother and a dog.

—parents divorced.

—brother and Marti live with Dad.

—Dad a commercial artist.

—Dad teaching at the private university here in town for one year.

The thing that amazes me the most is that she tells me all this without gasping for air once.

"I can't believe you don't run track," I finally say.

She shrugs.

"Not interested," she says.

The waterfalls are just ahead of us. "Look," I say, "we're almost there." For just a minute I wonder what it would feel like not to care what other people think. I wonder what it would feel like if I did things because *I* wanted to do them. Not Dad. Not Granddad. Not Coach. Just me, Cal Cameron.

After we run, I take her home and she invites me in. I am in for a major surprise.

Her dad is sitting at the kitchen table reading the newspaper. He's not a big guy at all, but still nice-looking. Full head of dark hair. Graying temples. Light-rimmed glasses. A gray turtleneck.

"Ah," he smiles as we walk through the door. Marti gives him a bear hug.

"Dad," she says, turning to me again, "this is Cal Cameron."

Mr. Jeffs stands up and shakes my hand. "Nice to meet you, Cal," he says.

"Where's Freddie?" Marti asks.

"Downstairs," says Mr. Jeffs, "waiting for *Monday Night Football* to start." He turns to me and explains. "Freddie is a serious football fanatic."

"Cal plays football, Dad," Marti says.

Mr. Jeffs smiles at me. "Well, Freddie will certainly want to be your friend, then."

"I'm going to get Freddie," says Marti. "Bring him up to say hi. Be back in a minute."

I stay behind and talk to Mr. Jeffs, who turns out to be a pretty nice guy. I find out he used to work for Marvel Comics. Mr. Jeffs did the lettering for a few of the *Amazing Spider-Man* adventures under the name of Griff (the 'Gator) Jeffs.

I should explain something here. I am a major superhero comic book fanatic. I always have been. Whenever Mom used to take me and Eugene to the library in the summer, I always headed straight for the magazine rack where this one really nice librarian kept a few comic books. So while Eugene sat in one corner of the library reading books about guys like Thomas Alva Edison—Eugene was Provo City Library's SuperStar Reader three years in a row—I sat in the other corner reading books about guys like Spider-Man. So when I find out Mr. Jeffs used to letter some of the Spider-Man adventures, I think this is nothing short of great.

Before long, Marti and Freddie join us. I don't mean to, but I stare.

"Cal," says Marti, "meet my brother Freddie."

Freddie is short—maybe five-three or five-four—and he's a little dumpy around the middle. He has freckles and thick glasses and light straight hair that sticks up in funny places. He has a turned-up nose and slanted eyes and thick lips. He doesn't look like Marti or like Marti's dad because —I can tell—Freddie is retarded.

"Hi, Freddie," I say.

Freddie steps forward, a big smile on his face. He's wearing a black jersey that says RAIDERS on the back. "How do you do?" He puts his hand out so I can give him five.

"Freddie," says Marti, "Cal plays football."

Freddie's eyes light up. He looks at me like I'm a real hero. "I want to play football, too," he says. "I want to be the quarterback."

"Cal's a quarterback, Freddie," says Marti.

"Yessir," says Mr. Jeffs. "You ought to see this kid's arm, Cal."

"Wanna play catch?" Freddie asks me. "I have a football."

"Yeah," I say. "That would be great." Actually, I feel pretty uncomfortable. I don't know. Can kids like Freddie catch a ball? Will I hurt him?

We all go out into the back yard. Marti and her dad sit on some patio chairs while I throw the ball to Freddie. I take it really easy on him, slinging the ball underarm a lot. He does okay, though, and if Boy wouldn't tackle Freddie everytime the ball comes their way he'd be doing a whole lot better. Also, he really does throw the ball pretty well. I mean, he throws it better than Eugene does. I guess I don't know what I was expecting.

"Okay, pretty good," I say. "This time go out on a pattern. Run straight back, then cut to your right."

"Okay!" Freddie takes off, crunching through the fallen leaves as fast as he can. He moves to the right and I heave the ball in his direction. He takes it right in the chest, then falls backward.

"Touchdown!" Marti's dad yells.

Freddie gets up, still hugging the ball. He has leaves on his jersey, leaves in his hair. Then he spikes the ball, just like in the pros.

"Penalty! Fine that man!" I yell.

Marti and her dad cheer. Boy knocks Freddie down again.

Afterward we all go back inside for Cokes. I watch part of the game on the TV with Freddie, but it's getting late and I have to go. I promised my dad I would bag leaves. As it is, I'll be bagging them under a full moon.

"I gotta be going," I say.

Freddie and Marti follow me to the door.

"Thanks, Cal," says Marti. "I had a nice time running with you."

"Yeah, me too."

" 'Bye, Cal," says Freddie.

I get an idea. "Hey, Freddie," I say, "what if I could get you a practice jersey?"

Well, I can see old Freddie is getting ready to enter me in his personal Hall of Fame. He practically does a dance in the doorway.

"That would be neat, Cal," he says. "Real neat!"

Marti looks over the top of his head and smiles at me. I smile back.

Before you get to thinking what a wonderful guy I am, though, I should tell you that I just about got ready to invite Freddie to a football practice.

But I didn't.

After that, Marti and I start running together a couple of times a week. I've even talked her into working on some kind of training program with me. I make her run all-out for short distances, for instance, then slow down again to an easier pace.

While we're running together, we talk about all kinds of things like what we want to do when we get out of school. Marti, for instance, has the next eight years pretty well set. First college, then veterinary school. When she asks me what I want to do I tell her I want to be Lee Iacocca's bodyguard.

"Come on," she says, "get serious."

"I am serious," I say.

"You know what your problem is?" she says.

"Which problem is that?" I say.

"You don't know the first thing about yourself."

"Now, that would be a very original observation if my dad, Coach, and any number of my teachers hadn't thought of it first."

"Well, that's my opinion, too."

"Doesn't it ever get boring," I tease, "having an opinion on everything?"

One day I ask her why she didn't tell me about Freddie when she told me about her family.

She shrugs. "What's to tell?"

"I don't know."

"Look, if I were to tell you that Freddie is mentally

retarded, that is what you would focus on right from the first. It's natural. Everyone does. If I don't say anything, people don't come to him with so many set ideas."

This makes sense to me. Maybe I would have been a lot less natural around Freddie the first time if I'd known about his handicap.

This whole Freddie business has helped me understand a lot of things. Like, for instance, I think I understand better why Marti hates guys like Sean. It's not hard to imagine that guys like him have hassled Freddie plenty of times. I'm just guessing, though. We've never discussed it.

Actually, we hardly ever discuss anyone or anything connected with school—except for Miss Tanner, the biology teacher, who Marti thinks is about the neatest teacher that ever lived.

It's funny, because I feel in some ways as though I'm living two lives. You know, Peter Parker by day, Spider-Man by night. There's my life at school and then there's my life after school. After hours I'm a real prince of a guy. I run with Marti. I have heart-to-hearts with her dad. I play with Freddie and teach him new defenses. Things like that.

At school, it's a different story. Call me a jerk, but I act like I hardly know her. Which isn't tough to do. We have only one class together. And I make sure I'm pretty busy afterward.

The fact is that Marti does not fit in at school—anywhere. She doesn't have any close friends except the Geekman and Miss Tanner and this girl named Rosie Stephens who has wild red hair and who writes murder mysteries during noon hour. Marti doesn't seem to care, though. She acts like she's better than everybody else. Her attitude can be very irritating—and I even like Marti.

7

A funny thing happens to me on the way out to football practice.

I'm in the locker room bathroom. While I'm sitting in my stall, I hear my name. This, as you can imagine, makes me want to listen. I hold my breath and I don't move.

Someone swears, then says, "What is going on with Cameron?"

I know that voice. It belongs to Sean. My good old buddy Sean.

"Don't ask me," someone answers. I'm not sure, but I think it's Craig Kennedy, another receiver.

Can you believe this? I'm being discussed and I'm around to hear it. I thought this happened only in the movies.

"Someone needs to tell him to pull his head out," Sean says. "Someone needs to tell him to pull his head out before the entire season is wasted." Sean is bugged. Really bugged. I don't need to see his face—I can hear it plain enough in his voice.

So what would you do if you heard yourself being discussed in the bathroom? Would you stroll out of the stall and try to make Sean feel like a jerk? Or would you hide until you were sure he was gone? Guess what I do.

I wait.

I wait until Sean and Craig are gone and then I let myself out. I'm shaking all over. I feel totally and completely sick to my stomach. The worst part is that I've got to face Sean again. Sean and Bear and I, we're going out tonight.

* * *

So here I am, waiting for Sean to pick me up in his mom's suburban. The three of us are taking Jennifer, Melissa, and Joy the Student Body to the Fright Palace.

Let me explain. The Fright Palace is an old barn by the lake that the Theater Department of the university turns into a haunted house every October. They stuff it full of cobwebs and bales of hay and fake skeletons. Then they dress up like spooks and run around the place wailing and moaning. Pretty terrifying, let me tell you. They charge admission and raise money for the March of Dimes.

Sean and Bear and I go to the Fright Palace every year. When we were in the seventh grade, Sean got picked up by the police for spraying two ghosts and a witch with a fire extinguisher. He didn't stay in trouble for long, though. He never does.

I'm the last person to be picked up. Jennifer's already in the car. I get in beside her.

"Hi," I say. Everyone answers. But the air feels a little chilly—and not because it's cold outside either.

"So what have you been doing?" Bear asks me.

Before I can answer, Sean says, "He hasn't been throwing footballs, that's for sure."

Everyone laughs a little nervously at this.

I feel like hitting Sean, if you want to know the truth. But I don't, naturally. I just look out the window instead. I can tell already that this is going to be one swell evening.

Sean drives down Center Street. I see Mr. Payne standing on the corner in front of Provo Paint, shaking his head and talking even though he's alone. I get the willies just looking at him, and I turn away.

Sean is quiet and so is Bear. The girls don't seem to notice. They keep talking. Joy the Student B. is telling us all about her gay hairdresser, Art. Jennifer is saying "Oofer gross" and flipping her bangs out of her eyes like she wants to throw them away. Melissa keeps giggling. I can't tell you how interesting I find all of this.

When we get to the Fright Palace, Sean docks the suburban.

"Now, you're sure this won't give you nightmares, aren't you, Cal?" Sean says.

Everyone gives a nervous little laugh—again. I feel eyes on me, watching me.

"Hey," I say, "don't worry about me, pal."

"You're sure, now," Sean says.

I would personally like to strangle Sean.

"Knock it off, Sean," Bear finally says.

We get out of the car and head for the Fright Palace. The blood is pounding in my ears.

Have you ever had the experience of feeling like an outsider with a group of people who are normally your friends? That's how I feel right now. I feel like a total loser. I can't think of anything to say and so I find myself hanging back a little. Watching. Not really participating.

I'm watching Sean in particular. He's giving everyone in costume a really bad time—shouting in their faces, pulling off their wigs, sitting in their laps. And he keeps asking me if my heart can take all the excitement. Of course everything he does makes Joy the Student B. squeal with laughter.

You know, I've just realized something that's pretty amazing. I don't think I like Sean very much. In some ways, he is kind of a jerk.

An hour or so passes and it's time to go. When we leave the Fright Palace, we see guess who. Marti and Wally Geke and Freddie are walking across the parking lot. It looks like somebody wrapped fifty ace bandages around Freddie so that he can pass for a mummy. Marti's wearing a sweatshirt with something written on it. The Geekman is no doubt whistling the theme song from *The Addams Family*.

They don't see us.

"Hey!" Sean laughs and points. "Look at the freak show!"

Did I say I don't like Sean much? The fact is that right now I hate him. I hate the way he looks, the way he talks, the way he acts. I especially hate the way he treats people.

If I had any guts, I'd stand up to Sean. I'd tell him what I think. I'd tell him that I never want anything to do with him again.

But I don't. I just look the other way. And I really pray that Marti doesn't see me.

I feel so guilty about ignoring Marti at the Fright Palace that I ignore her some more. Does that make sense to you? For the next few days at school, I avoid her.

One day she stops by my locker.

"Hi," Marti says.

"Hi yourself."

We just sort of stand there until I say "Interesting sweatshirt." Actually her shirt makes me a little uncomfortable. It says A WOMAN NEEDS A MAN LIKE A FISH NEEDS A BICYCLE. I wonder where Marti gets these things. I don't think you can get them here in Provo.

"Thanks," Marti says. Then she looks at me. "Have I said something stupid again?"

"No."

"Oh," she shrugs. "I get the feeling you're avoiding me."

Bingo.

"No. I'm not," I lie. "Even if I were, it would have nothing to do with you." Stupid, stupid. Marti looks at me sideways.

"Here," I say, remembering something. I fish around in my locker for a minute. Then I pull out a practice jersey. "This is for Freddie."

Marti doesn't take it. Instead she just looks at it dangling from my hand. "Bring it to the house and give it to him yourself," she says finally. Then she walks away.

I go to Marti's house after practice. I stick Freddie's jersey in my gym bag. I also put in a stopwatch. I have a plan.

When I get to the house, Freddie opens the door. He goes nuts when he sees me.

"Cal!"

"Freddie!"

We give each other high five.

"I have a present for you, Freddie."

"Oh, wow," he says.

I put the bag on the floor and open it up. Freddie crouches over.

"Here you go, buddy." I pull out the jersey.

"Oh, wow!" he says again. "Dad! Dad!" Freddie runs off.

Marti walks into the room. She stops for just a second, like she's surprised to see me. It's about the first time I've ever seen Marti surprised. She's like a cat in a way. You have a hard time putting one over on a cat, but when you do, it looks so off-balance, so ridiculous almost.

"Oh!" she says. "I didn't hear the doorbell."

"Freddie let me in," I tell her. "I came over to give him the jersey."

Marti recovers herself. She gives me that sly smile of hers. "Better than Santa Claus, aren't you?"

"No doubt about it," I say.

We talk for a little while in the living room. Freddie runs in to show me how he looks in his new jersey. Then he disappears again.

"And now," I say, looking directly at Marti, "you and I are going to do something new tonight."

"Oh?" She arches an eyebrow.

"Yeah. Go get your sweats on."

Marti does and I tell her that we're getting in the car. She calls for Boy, but I tell her to leave Boy home this time. I can see she's thinking about arguing for a minute, but then changes her mind. I guess curiosity has gotten the best of her.

I drive her to the school.

"What are we doing here?" she wants to know.

"You'll see."

We park the car in the east parking lot and walk toward the football field. No one's around. A few stray leaves blow across the sidelines. The sky has turned gray. It will be dark soon.

Our football field is surrounded by a track. This is where we go.

"Here we are," I say, dropping my gym bag on the track.

Marti stares at me for a minute, her head tilted to the side. "This is where we're running tonight?"

"No," I say, "this is where *you're* running tonight."

Before she has a chance to tell me to go jump, I explain. "I just want to see how fast you can go." I stoop over the bag and pull out the stopwatch.

"This," says Marti, still staring at me, "is stupid."

"Aw, come on, Martha," I say. "Aren't you the least bit curious? Don't you want to know how fast you can run a mile?"

"No."

"Well, I want to know."

Marti is just staring at me. I think she may even be a little mad.

"Please oh please oh please oh please." I use my whiny voice—the one that cracks up my mom and makes Eugene crazy.

Still Marti doesn't say anything, although she is smiling a little now.

"If you don't run around the track I'll take Freddie's jersey away."

"Bully," says Marti.

I shrug, just to convince her that ice flows in these veins.

"Okay," she says. "You win."

Marti begins to warm up. She bends over, stretching out the backs of her calves.

"Of course this whole episode will be strictly unofficial," I tell her.

"Strictly," Marti grunts.

"So if you break any state records here this evening they won't count."

"Absolutely not," she puffs.

"It wouldn't be fair."

"No, it wouldn't be fair."

I feel myself rolling here. "It wouldn't be fair to all those good little girls who have worked so hard, who have sweated so much, who have yearned so intensely, to have their glory snatched from them by someone who doesn't even care."

Marti stands up. "Cal," she says, "shut up."

She runs up and back the stretch a few times.

"Ready?" I finally ask.

"Okay."

She peels off her sweats, jogs in place for a minute, then gets ready to take off.

"On your mark, get set, go!"

Marti takes off. She starts out at a steady even clip and gets stronger with each lap. I yell her splits at her each time she passes. Marti is getting incredible times.

I can't believe the time she's getting, to tell you the honest truth. I mean she is flying. She's even better than I thought she was.

"Go, Marti!" I scream at her. "Come on. That's the way!"

As you can see, I am practically turning into my grand-dad here.

She comes down the final stretch. Her stride is even, her arms are pumping, her hair flies out behind her like a yellow flag. She looks beautiful. Just beautiful.

Marti steps over the finish line. I stop the watch. I can't believe what I see. "Hey!" I shout. "Come look at this!"

Marti staggers over to me. Her cheeks are bright red. I can see her breath in the cold evening air. I hand the stop-watch to her. She takes it, looks at it. Her head comes up quickly and she looks at me.

"Really?" she says quietly.

I nod. "You are nothing short of terrific. Honest."

And then I do something that surprises us both. I lift her right off her feet and hug her hard.

She laughs at first, then we look at each other. I let her down slowly. She lifts her chin, and I kiss her.

When I get home, I find Granddad in the kitchen.

"Where've you been, laddie?"

I shrug. "Oh, around." I go to the fridge and open it up. I am practically overjoyed to find a box of unopened Ding Dongs in there. This is certainly my lucky day. I take out the box and give it a little flip while humming a little tune. This is what happens to people who hang around with Wally Geke too long.

"Feeling happy, are we?" says my mom, walking into the kitchen. She sees the box of Ding Dongs and slaps my hand. "After dinner, you."

"Aw, Mom."

"Hope you're planning on being around tonight," she says, ignoring my pleas for Ding Dongs. "Granddad's found some old films he wants to show us."

Ordinarily this would not thrill me. Granddad is the kind of guy who considers himself a real first-rate photographer. And it is true that he takes a zillion pictures and movies and (now) videos. But he takes them of such strange things. Like when he went on a trip to Hawaii with the Silver Seniors he took videos of the interior of an empty cafeteria at the Polynesian Cultural Center. Stuff like that. You look at the video and you sort of wonder what was going through Granddad's mind when he shot it.

But I am in such a good mood, such a swell mood, such a terrific mood that I'd sit through reruns of *Gilligan's Island* with Wally Geke right now.

I'm in the front room helping Granddad set up the projector when I hear my dad come in through the kitchen door.

"Your dad's here. With old home movies," I hear my mom say.

My dad says something that sounds a lot like "holy shit." I practically drop a reel. Let me explain. My father doesn't swear. Weird, I know, but he doesn't. He acts like it's against the law for dentists to swear. So when he walks through the kitchen and says "holy shit" in front of my mom, I naturally react.

Granddad, who doesn't hear much unless you're making direct eye contact with him anyway, doesn't respond.

"Okay, laddie," he says. "Here we go." He calls my parents. "Sandy! MaryBeth! We're ready."

My mom walks into the living room with the smile she uses at unpleasant events like parent-teacher conferences. My dad follows her, looking pretty miserable. Granddad doesn't see any of this.

He turns to me. "Okay, laddie. Lights."

I turn off the lights. The film rattles through the machine. First numbers, then moving pictures, appear on the screen.

The movies are old, like before my time. My dad is standing on Granddad's front lawn. He's toothbrush thin, with an Adam's apple that bulges. He wears thick glasses with black frames and he looks nervous. To tell you the truth, he looks a little like Mister Rogers.

"Hee hee," my granddad laughs. "Look at your arms there, Sandy."

My mom holds up one of my dad's arms and examines it closely. "You've filled out since then, crusher." Then she puts her arm around his shoulders and snuggles closer. My dad manages a minor smile.

Onscreen my dad is joined by a big, beefy kind of guy with so many teeth you'd think he was Donny Osmond or maybe Ted Kennedy.

My mother gasps.

Though I never knew him—he died in Vietnam—I know the man on the screen is my uncle Robert. Uncle Robert grabs my dad around the neck and accidentally knocks his glasses off. Though you can't hear anything, you can see that the two of them are laughing.

"What a lad," my granddad says.

We watch the rest of the reel, pictures of Dad and Uncle Robert horsing around—Uncle Robert throwing a ball at my dad, Dad dropping it.

It gets really quiet in the living room. It's like we've invited a ghost to dinner.

Finally the movie ends. There are other reels, but Granddad doesn't move to pick them up. Everybody acts glued to their seats. Finally he says, "I'm tired. I think I'll go home."

My mom springs to her feet. "That's a good idea, Dad. I think we're all a little tired tonight. Here, let me help you with those."

Granddad and my mom gather up the films. I unplug and wind the projector cord. My dad doesn't do anything, but stares straight ahead.

That night as I try to go to sleep, I can't get the picture

of my dad and Uncle Robert out of my mind. I hear my
mom shuffling in her carpet slippers down the hallway.

"Mom?"

She backtracks and pokes her head in my door.

"Hi."

"Mom," I say, "why did you marry Dad?"

She steps all the way inside now.

"Because he asked me to," she says. Ordinarily I would
have thrown a pillow or something at her, but tonight I'm
too tired, too sad to move. She giggles a little, then walks
across the room and sits down on the end of my bed.

"Why do you want to know?"

I shrug. "You two seem so different," I say finally.

"We are in many ways," she says slowly, "which is
probably why I fell in love with your father. I liked his
quietness, his gentleness. I liked his brains. I still do. And
then he's always laughed at my jokes."

We don't say anything. A car passes by outside and
makes shadows on my wall.

"Did Dad love Uncle Robert?"

My mom thinks about this for a minute.

"He was jealous of him in some ways, I suppose," she
says. "Your granddad made no secret about the fact that he
preferred Robert. But yes, he did love your uncle Robert.
A lot. When your uncle Robert was listed as missing in
action, well . . ." she doesn't finish, just shakes her head.

"What was he like? Uncle Robert, I mean."

"Oh," my mom says, "he was a lot like you."

That's what I thought she would say somehow, because
when I looked at the films, it was like looking at a moving
picture of myself in funny clothes.

I'm trying to grab hold of an idea here. It has something
to do with my dad and me, about why we don't get along.
I wonder. When my dad looks at me, does he see Uncle
Robert?

For some reason my heart feels as heavy as rocks.

* * *

So now I'm sitting here in English class. Bear's looking at Miss Shumway like he's really interested in what she's saying about verbs being so active they practically jump around, except that he's sticking pencils in his ears. You ought to see Bear. The pencils are standing straight out from the side of his head. Everyone's looking at him. Everyone's smiling. Sean is laughing out loud. But Bear keeps a totally straight face, which is pretty incredible when you think about it. Miss Shumway is trying to ignore him. This is her new strategy for dealing with us. She pretends like we're not even in the same universe with her.

Me, I'm sitting here thinking about last night's home movies.

I can't figure this out. It's not like the movies were anything special. Nobody's going to die if Granddad doesn't get an Oscar in the spring, for example. And it's not like I haven't seen pictures of my dad and Uncle Robert before. It's just that the sight of them together—Uncle Robert looking like something out of a book on Greek mythology, Dad looking like the secretary-treasurer of Wimps Anonymous—got to me this time. I mean *really* got to me. Last night after Mom left my room I just lay there in my bed trying to get comfortable and turning my pillow over every time it got too hot. I don't know about you, but one thing I definitely cannot stand are hot sheets and pillowcases.

As you can tell, I'm in a real swell mood.

More and more people are laughing now. Just like Sean. The whole world wants to be just like Sean.

The bell rings. Everyone gets up and starts walking out, even though Miss Shumway is saying "I did not dismiss you. I DID NOT dismiss you."

I'm slow getting up. I feel someone standing over my desk. It's Marti.

"Hi," she says with a half smile.

I hate myself, but I look out of the corner of my eye to see if anyone's watching us. No one is. Sean and Bear are gone.

"Hi yourself," I say.

"I'm sore this morning," she says. "Running like that last night really took it out of me."

Now it's my turn to smile. "Hey, Jeffs," I say, just like I'm Coach, "sometimes pushing yourself to be better hurts."

"No pain, no gain. Right?"

"That's what they tell me," I say.

Marti checks her watch. "Gotta go," she says. "I'm meeting Rosie in the library. Maybe I'll be around again tonight. With me you never know."

We walk out of the room together.

To tell you the truth, at this very minute I'm not thinking about Dad and Uncle Robert anymore.

Have you ever noticed how sometimes you go along for a while when nothing much happens? Then that suddenly changes and everything starts happening at once?

Take tonight, for instance. Mom's in the kitchen getting dinner ready. Dad's busy reading all the really boring parts of the newspaper, like the obituaries. My dad just loves to read the obituaries. He likes to see if any of his patients have dropped dead recently so that he can get his receptionist Annemarie to send flowers. Naturally he never reads the sports pages.

And then there's Eugene the G. Home for the weekend. Like the guy is in college and he still can't figure out what to do with himself on a Friday night except sit on a sofa and watch something educational on PBS. Which is exactly what Eugene's doing right now. He's watching something about insects, if you can believe it.

The kitchen door slams and I hear my mother say, "Hi, Dad. How are you tonight? Stay for dinner?"

It's Granddad.

My granddad gives a brief snort, which is his way of saying yes. You may have noticed that Granddad is not exactly long on small talk.

Granddad leaves the kitchen and walks into the front room, where Dad and Eugene and I are all sitting. I can tell just by looking at him that he's in a foul mood, that he's looking for a reason to chew somebody up into little tiny bits. Granddad, as they say, is spoiling for a fight.

He starts in on Dad first.

"Sandy," he says, throwing out his jaw, "have you collected that money Dale Moon owes you?"

Dale Moon, another Silver Senior, is my granddad's archrival. My granddad has never beaten him at bowling. Not even once. This naturally makes my granddad crazy. Dad works on Mr. Moon's teeth, even though Mr. Moon never bothers to pay down his account.

This makes my granddad even crazier. He sort of believes you have the right to seriously injure people who owe you money.

"Well?" My granddad says. "Has Dale paid you?"

My dad keeps his nose parked in the middle of the paper. "No, Pop," he says. "Dale hasn't paid me yet."

Granddad practically falls to pieces in the middle of the living room floor, he's so irritated.

"Get some backbone, man," he spits.

"Backbone," says my dad, turning a page. "I'll have Annemarie pick me up one tomorrow."

I'm amazed. My dad has just made a little joke.

Even Granddad can see that he won't be getting my dad's goat tonight. Lucky for him, there's still Eugene. My granddad just loves to pick on Eugene. He always has.

He squints his eyes and looks at Eugene. Then he looks at the TV. On the screen there's a shot of two moths crawling all over each other. Granddad looks at Eugene again. You can predict what happens next.

"Now, why on God's earth are you watching this, laddie?"

Eugene turns around and blinks a couple of times just like he's returned to planet Earth after an extended leave of absence.

"Oh," says Eugene, which is what he always says when he finally notices that other people are in the same room with him. Only he says it through really tight little lips so that his mouth looks exactly like a Cheerio right there in the middle of his face. The way he holds his lips when he says "oh" is just one of the many things that bothers me about Eugene.

"Oh," says Eugene again. "Hi, Granddad. I didn't see you standing there."

A major storm system is moving across Granddad's face. "I asked you why you canna manage to find something better than this."

Eugene just blinks.

So Granddad struts over to the TV and starts flipping through channels.

"Hey!" says Eugene. "Hey!"

But Granddad just keeps racing through the channels until he finds something he wants to watch. I'll give you a hint. It isn't about moths.

Me, I just keep my head buried in *Sports Illustrated*.

The doorbell rings.

"Get that, will you, Cal," my dad says.

I groan, but I get up and answer the door.

It's Marti.

"Hi," she says.

My stomach does a back dive.

"Hi," I say. She's wearing jeans and the sweatshirt I told you about—the one that says

A WOMAN NEEDS A MAN LIKE A FISH NEEDS A BICYCLE.

Marti shifts her weight, then laughs a little. "I've got something for you. A little surprise. Can I come in?" She's got that little half smile on her face.

I feel like a total jerk for making her stand around on my front porch.

"Sorry. Come in."

Marti walks into the family room. My dad looks up and sees her. He smiles and stands up.

"Well, hello there," he says. "You're Cal's friend." Like she doesn't know who she is or something.

"Right." Marti smiles and stretches out her hand so my dad can shake it. "Marti Jeffs."

"Sure," my dad says. "I remember." He's staring at her teeth, admiring her enamel no doubt.

Of course by now Eugene and Granddad are looking at Marti, too. I figure it's time to make introductions,

"Marti," I say, holding my breath, "this is my brother Eugene."

This is what happens to guys who hang out in honors biology classes too long. They can't figure out what to do with a girl unless she happens to be a newt or maybe a fruit fly. I'll say this for Eugene, though. At least he has better personal grooming habits than a lot of his buddies. Eugene has always flossed regularly. You got to give the guy credit for that.

Of course I wait for Eugene to say something totally stupid, like "I'm the good-looking one."

"I'm the good-looking one," Eugene says, then laughs.

Marti smiles and says, "Nice to meet you."

Granddad is trying to get a good look, too. I'm hoping he won't notice the sweatshirt. He won't get it, which will make him totally crazy.

"And this is Granddad," I say, feeling a little nervous.

"Hi," says Marti.

Granddad squints and mumbles a greeting. Then he

turns to the TV again. Like I say, Granddad is a black eye just waiting to happen this evening.

Marti and I sit down on the couch. She hands me a sack. Inside there's a framed drawing of Spider-Man. It's autographed: "For our good friend Cal. Best Wishes, Griffin Jeffs."

"Wow!" I say, sounding a little like Wally Geke. "Thanks. Tell your dad thanks."

Mom walks into the living room. "Dinner, everyone!" She stops when she sees Marti.

"Mom," I say, "this is a friend of mine. Marti Jeffs."

I'll tell you right now that old Mom looks pretty surprised. For one thing, she's never heard me talk about Marti. Weird, I know, but it's like Marti is my secret, part of another life. Or at least she used to be.

"Hello, Marti." Mom gives me a look with an eyebrow raised just like a question mark. She's got a little smile on her face—kind of knowing. Kind of like Marti, as a matter of fact.

"Why don't you stay for dinner," Mom says. "Cal, go set an extra plate, please."

I go into the kitchen, where I can see my worst nightmares are about to come true. My mom may be a lot of things, but a good cook she ain't.

Tonight, for instance, we're having lime gelatin, carrot sticks, and her specialty—SpaghettiOs with little slices of hot dog in it. Mom calls it MaryBeth Cameron's Hot Dog Delight. It's definitely not the kind of thing you feed a girl you'd like to impress.

Mom comes into the kitchen.

"Geez, Mom," I whisper. "Hot dogs?"

She burns me with a glance. "You," she says, "can just be quiet."

Everyone else trickles in and we sit around the table.

"Oh, great," Eugene says. "SpaghettiOs!" Only he's not making a joke. Eugene loves SpaghettiOs. He thinks

SpaghettiOs are one of the World's Ten Most Important Inventions. I avoid looking at Marti.

We start to eat. Marti asks Eugene what he's doing these days and he tells her about school and how he's already a lab assistant even though he's only a freshman. It's hard to believe what a boring guy Eugene can be at times. But Marti acts like she's interested, and you can tell Eugene thinks Marti is the greatest thing since software.

"What does it say?" Granddad blurts out.

Eugene stops talking. We all look at each other.

"What do you mean, Dad," Mom finally says.

"Her shirt," Granddad says. "What does it say?"

Everyone looks at Marti. Things get real quiet. Marti reads from her sweatshirt. "It says 'A woman needs a man like a fish needs a bicycle.'" Marti looks up and smiles.

Eugene and my dad just stare at her. Mom bursts out laughing. She and Marti smile at each other.

"What?" says my granddad. "Now what does she mean by that?" He asks my mom.

From the way she's playing with her fork, I think Marti may actually be a little nervous. But you'd never know it from the look on her face or the sound of her voice.

"Well," she tells my grandfather, "it's a joke, obviously. But the idea behind it is serious. It just means a woman doesn't need a man to be happy."

"Amen!" my mother practically shouts. I get the feeling she's enjoying this in some weird way. My granddad gets ready to say something else, but Mom manages to distract him with another helping of Hot Dog Delight.

I clear my throat. "You know, Marti here is an excellent runner."

"Is that right," says my dad. He smiles at her.

I tell everyone about Marti's time at the track last night. Eugene acts all impressed, even though he wouldn't know a good time from a bad one. To my surprise, Marti blushes.

Granddad comes up for air. "The lassie runs, eh?" He looks at Eugene. "Did you hear that? Cal says the lassie runs."

"Yes," says Eugene. "I think that's just wonderful." He beams at Marti.

Granddad is still looking at Eugene. Then he snorts. "I'd not be a bit surprised if she can run faster than you, laddie."

Nobody says a word. To tell you the truth, we're all in a state of shock that Granddad would say something like that about Eugene in front of Marti, even if it's probably true.

Finally my dad speaks up, "Oh for Pete's sake, Pop."

"Well, look at him there," my granddad says in a very loud voice. "All he cares about are books. Books, books, books. It isn't natural."

My mother looks like she would personally love to strangle Granddad.

"I'll say it again." Granddad's voice is getting really high. "It isn't natural."

I look at Marti from the corner of my eye. She's watching us all, just like a cat on a windowsill.

It gets worse. Granddad starts badgering Eugene, really picking on him, practically calling him a sissy right there in front of Marti.

And Eugene, Eugene the G., just sits there blinking, his face bright red. He's trying to smile, but he looks like he just might cry instead.

I tell you what. Suddenly I feel sick inside.

"Hey, Granddad," I say quietly. "Lay off."

Granddad jerks his head around and looks at me. So does everyone else for that matter.

"You heard me. Leave my brother alone."

Granddad's eyes open wide. He looks surprised. Surprised and hurt as a little kid.

Nobody says much after that. When we finally finish

dinner, I offer to take Marti home in the nerdmobile. But we don't go straight home. I drive her up the canyon, my window opened just a crack so I can feel cold air slap my hot face. Like I said before, I always drive up here when I want to forget how I'm feeling.

We drive for miles and I don't say a word.

"Your granddad," Marti says after a while. "Is he always like that?"

I change my grip on the steering wheel and shrug. "My grandfather is a very old guy who also happens to be the president of the Cal Cameron Fan Club. What can I say?"

"Is he always so hard on Eugene?"

"No"—which is the truth— "but he does like to pick on him. My brother, you may have noticed, is a very easy guy to pick on."

Suddenly I start thinking about those stupid home movies again and I feel the bitterness collect in a hard little lump at the back of my throat. I can actually *taste* how bad I'm feeling right now.

"It's the same old stupid pattern over and over and over again," I say. Outside, an unending line of pine trees streams past us.

I tell Marti about Dad and about Uncle Robert. "And so now Granddad has turned me and Eugene into his sons all over again. Frankly, I don't know how Eugene's put up with it. I don't know how my dad put up with it either."

We keep driving. No noise now but the rush of canyon wind screaming through my window.

"You want to hear something funny?" I finally say. Only you can tell from my voice that what I have to say isn't really funny at all.

"What's that, Cal?" Marti says in a low voice. In the dark I can feel her bright eyes on me.

"I'm jealous of Eugene. Can you believe it? A swell guy like me jealous of a nerd like Eugene? I'm jealous of my brother because our father loves him better than he loves me." Just like my grandfather loved Uncle Robert more than he loved my dad. Another old pattern. Over and over.

I have no idea why I'm talking like this, why I'm telling Marti these things. I'm probably making a royal fool out of myself. But tonight I don't care. Tonight I don't give a damn.

Suddenly I feel tired. "My dad. He must have hated my uncle Robert sometimes. I don't blame him."

Outside, the moon breaks free from the tops of trees and shines through the window on Marti's hair.

"He probably did hate him," Marti says slowly. "Hated him and loved him, too."

Then she turns her face so I can't see it and I get the feeling that Marti is lost in some private pain of her own.

8

Marti and I have started spending a lot of time together, mostly at her house. I'll go over there and her dad will build a fire with plenty of help from Freddie. Then we'll sit around the basement there and play games like 221B Baker Street. Marti and her dad are real Sherlock Holmes fans. They've read every single Arthur Conan Doyle story at least twice. I don't know how much Freddie understands when they read the stories aloud to each other, but he does have a blue Siamese fighting fish named Dr. Watson.

Tonight on Marti's front porch I hear voices inside. Loud voices. It sounds like Marti and her dad are having a fight. Actually, Marti is the one doing most of the shouting.

"I don't understand you," I hear her say.

"This does not really concern you. It's between your mother and me," Mr. Jeffs tells her.

I don't know what to do. To tell you the truth, hearing Marti and her dad go at each other makes me a little uncomfortable. Usually they're such terrific pals. I decide that maybe this isn't the greatest time for a visit. I turn to leave and find Freddie and Boy standing right behind me.

"Hiya, Freddie. I didn't hear you come up the stairs."

Boy jumps up and slobbers on me a few times. Freddie smiles. "Wanna see my rock collection, Cal?" What can I say? So Freddie and I go inside.

Walking in on a family argument is one of my least favorite experiences—right up there with listening to the Geekman recite all fifty state capitals backwards and forwards in two minutes or less while waiting to buy lunch tickets. Marti has two bright pink spots burning in the middle of her cheeks. Mr. Jeffs looks like he just spent the night sleeping on a bus.

"Hi," I say, feeling very out of place.

Mr. Jeffs is the first one to pull himself together. He looks at me and smiles.

"Cal, hi. Forgive us. Marti and I were having a—discussion."

"I know," I say with a little smile of my own. "I heard."

This makes Mr. Jeffs laugh. Marti just glares at us both.

"I've got to run some errands. I'll take Freddie with me," he tells Marti. "We'll continue our discussion later."

"No we won't," she snaps. "I don't have anything more to say."

I look at Marti's dad and shrug. "I'm sorry, Mr. Jeffs, but you heard what Marti said. No more discussions. Ever."

You may want to know why I keep talking like this. It's because I'm nervous, and when I'm nervous, my mouth switches to automatic. At least Mr. Jeffs seems to think I'm funny. He shakes his head and laughs. "I see you understand how my daughter operates," he says. Then he puts his arm around Marti's shoulder and pulls her toward him. "Love you, babe," he says softly before he goes.

Marti stays stiff as a board as she watches him and Freddie leave.

I let out a low whistle. "What's going on here?"

Marti doesn't answer at first, and for a minute I think she's going to tell me it's none of my business.

"It's him" she finally blurts out.

"Your dad?" I say, a little surprised. "What's the matter with him?"

"He's just so—so *stubborn* sometimes!"

I think you'll agree this sounds pretty funny coming from Marti. I even smile a little. Lucky for me, Marti isn't looking at my face.

"Stubborn?" I say. "Actually, your dad seems like a pretty easygoing kind of a guy to me." In fact he seems a little too easygoing, a little too tolerant. Sometimes you worry that if Mr. Jeffs gets any more open-minded, his brains will start to fall out. I like the guy a lot, but he does strike me that way at times.

"You're right. He's usually a very easygoing guy, a very sensible guy," Marti admits, "but about this he's being totally unreasonable."

I wait for details.

"He's going to San Francisco this weekend to be with my mother," she finally tells me.

"Are they getting back together?"

"NO!" Marti practically screams.

It suddenly hits me that Marti never says anything about her mother. Never. Not even an "I got a letter from my mom yesterday." It's like Marti's mother doesn't even exist.

I look at her closely and I can see that she's really upset. If this were daytime television, now would be the perfect time for me to say "Do you want to talk about it?" Soap stars are always telling each other to talk about it. It's their mental-health motto. But with Marti I decide to keep my mouth shut for the moment. I figure if she wants to talk about it, she will.

"Sorry," says Marti finally. "I didn't mean to yell at you."

"Hey." I shrug. "It's okay."

"Want to go downstairs?" Marti asks. "Dad built a fire."

"Sure."

We go downstairs and stretch out in front of the hearth. Boy joins us. Marti doesn't take her eyes off the flames, but she begins to talk.

"My parents have what is known as an amicable divorce." Marti says the word "amicable" like it has a bad taste. "They keep in touch. She called last night and said she needed Dad's help. Wants him to make posters or something for another stupid demonstration she's organizing to save the whales. Whales are her latest cause. So naturally Dad drops everything and makes arrangements to go. Actually he's still hung up on her. He keeps holding out hope that they'll get back together one day."

"Do you want your parents to get back together?" I ask. I think I've already guessed the answer.

"No," says Marti.

"Do you think they will?"

"No," Marti says again.

"Then why don't you want your dad to go to San Francisco?"

"Because I hate what seeing my mother does to him. He can't say no to her. He's never been able to. So she'll use him up, tell him what a dear *friend* he is, then send him back on the airplane in a million little pieces. I would just like to spare him that. Is that so wrong?"

"He's a big boy now, Marti," I say slowly. "Maybe you ought to let him make that decision for himself."

Marti shoots me a look of total disgust. A log pops in the fireplace. Boy lifts his head for a minute, then sets it down on his paws again. I have a lot of questions, only I don't know how to ask them. Finally I settle on one.

"If your dad still loves your mom, then why did they get a divorce?"

"Because she needed her freedom, she said. She needed *space* to find out who she really is and what she really believes in, she said. She never had the chance, poor baby, what with her parents being the way they are and what with her marrying Dad when she was so young. Dad's a wonderful guy, she said, but this was just something she had to do and surely we could all understand that, couldn't we?

"You should have seen her, Cal. She worked up real tears and everything for the occasion. I just told her if she needed her freedom so badly that Freddie and I would be more than happy to stay with Dad. She got this pained look on her face like *I'd* hurt *her* feelings. 'Whatever you want, sweetheart,' she said. Can you believe that? Can you believe she had the nerve to say something like that to me?"

I shrug. How would I feel, what would I say, if my own mom decided to walk? To tell you the truth, I can't imagine her leaving, ever. She doesn't seem like the type. But then my mom's never been really unhappy at home either. "Do you hear from her? Talk to her?"

"I don't read her letters and I don't take her calls."

The way Marti says this almost gives me the creeps. She looks so fierce, so unforgiving—just like that kestrel Danny Petersen pulled down from the sky. To tell you the truth, I'd hate to have Marti get really mad at me. For a minute I even feel a little sorry for her mother.

"Come on," I say in a soft voice, "anybody who wants to save the whales can't be all bad."

I'm thinking of a program about whales I once watched with Eugene on PBS. The narrator talked about the whales like they were his best friends. He called them gentle giants, and he said they were dying because nobody cared. I don't think I'll ever forget the long and lonely sounds those whales made as they rose, then slipped into the sea.

"Saving whales," I say thinking out loud. "That sounds like something you'd do, Marti."

Marti levels me to the ground with a single stare. "Just for your information, Cal Cameron," she says, "my mother and I are nothing alike."

Then she turns her head quickly and stares into the flames. But not until I've seen her eyes shining with tears.

The Bear meets me at my locker first thing in the morning.

"I gotta talk to you, Cal," He says. He looks upset.

"Yeah? What's the matter?"

"It's Sean, Cal."

I can feel myself getting a little clammy, just like the way I used to feel when I had to give an oral report in front of the class when I was in the sixth grade. "What about Sean?"

Bear shoves his hands deep into his pockets. "Well, in case you haven't noticed, he's been on your case lately."

I shrug. "I've noticed." I slam my locker shut, and Bear and I walk down the hall together to our first-period class.

"He's been telling guys you're a loser, Cal. He says it's your fault that we haven't won more games this year."

"What does the guy want?" I say. "We're in the playoffs."

"Barely."

"So who cares? Past games don't matter now. Everybody starts with a clean slate for playoffs."

"Sure," says Bear, "but Sean says that doesn't matter, because you'll just screw up anyway."

"What a neat friend. A swell pal."

"Sean is—Sean. He always says what he thinks," says Bear. That's the Bear for you. He's loyal to me, no question, but he's loyal to Sean, too. Eugene used to say that Mike Mangum is a basically decent human being who, unfortunately, has noodles for brains. That's Eugene's evaluation, not mine. The Bear is okay.

"Sure he does," I say. "It just bothers me that when he says what he thinks he's usually saying it behind my back."

Bear looks really distressed.

So. There you have it. We are playing in the first game of the playoffs this afternoon. Dillon is starting, but I know Coach is planning on having me right there if things don't work out.

Sometimes I think Coach has made a mistake in the way he's handled the whole thing between Dillon and me. I think a coach probably ought to decide who's going to be his man and then stick with him no matter how he plays. This switching off between quarters—not to mention games—is too confusing, too unsettling. No one knows what's coming next. No one has any confidence.

It's a miracle to me, quite frankly, that we've even made the playoffs. We pulled out the last few games in the final quarter and we've squeaked our way into the playoffs. No one is counting on us—on me—to do much.

"Come on," I say to Bear. "Let's go to class."

Everyone is real nervous in the locker room right before the game. You can see it in their faces, in the way they move, in the way they talk to each other.

The Geekman is driving me crazy. He keeps punching me in the arm and saying "Yeah!" For some reason he believes this is pumping me up when in point of fact it's merely driving me nuts. That and giving me a sore arm.

The Geekman flits over to me again.

"Do *not* touch me," I warn him.

"Yeah!" He punches my arm.

Have you ever noticed that the people with very few friends like Wally Geke are usually that way because they keep doing obnoxious things?

"I mean it, Geke, leave me alone."

"Playoffs! Playoffs! Playoffs!" He starts whistling a little tune—one of his own, I imagine.

"Get outta here, Geke. I want it quiet."

He shifts into his Skipper routine. "Okay, little buddy,"

he says. Then he salutes—which of course makes me want to strangle him—and bounds off.

I close my eyes and lean against my locker. I visualize the different routes the receivers run. Then I watch myself taking the snap from the center and dropping back. One Two Three. I hit my tight end, who goes into the end zone for a touchdown. Eugene called me from Salt Lake last night to tell me that if you imagine yourself doing something like you were on video or something, you improve your chances for performing better. This sounds like something Eugene picked up at a star show, but I'm giving it a try.

When I open my eyes, I see that Sean is staring at me from across the aisle. I stare back. Sean doesn't do anything, doesn't say anything.

I'll say this for Sean. He wants to win. And he deserves to win, too, because he has worked harder than anyone else on the team. Where football is concerned, Sean is totally serious. He knows what he wants.

I look away.

"Okay!" Coach's voice roars through the locker room. "Out on the field!"

"Hey, Cameron," someone behind me says. I turn around. It's Dillon. He's standing there, his helmet still in his hand.

"Yeah?"

He doesn't say anything.

"Move it! Move it!" Coach is barking commands.

I throw out my hand and grab his. "Hey, buddy," I say. "Good luck!"

Dillon puts on his helmet and we trot out onto the field together.

There's nothing like a playoff game. For one thing, somebody besides the cheerleaders and my grandfather show up. All the kids—the soshes, the D-wingers, the debaters, the librarians—they all show up. And they all act like they're personally going to die if you don't the win the game. So there's lots of noise. Lots of excitement.

We go through warmups on the field. I have butterflies in my stomach. No doubt about it.

It's perfect football weather—cold and sunny—a real autumn day.

It's time for the school song. We move off the field onto the sidelines. The band marches out and plays a rousing rendition of "Fight, Ye Mighty Buffalo." Good enough to put a little starch into the shorts, even. Eugene, who used to play the tuba, would be impressed.

The clock on the scoreboard is counting away the minutes before the beginning of the game. The score is even. Home 0, Visitors 0.

The band moves off the field and the teams line up, ready for the kickoff. We receive. The ref blows his whistle and the game begins.

This is how the game goes. We get off to a quick start. After moving the ball downfield to the ten yard line, Dillon throws a screen pass to Sean, who runs over a few linemen and takes the ball into the end zone. A spectacular start, you might say.

After that, things start to fall apart. We get burned on one long pass play and we fumble on our own twenty yard line. That gives the other team two quick scores. Then they score a touchdown and a field goal. By the time the half rolls around the score is 24 to 7. It's obvious that the pressure of the playoff atmosphere has gotten to Dillon. He looks totally shell-shocked.

People ask me sometimes what happens in a locker room during the half. Does Coach get up and do a Knute Rockne or what? Actually, he hardly says anything inspirational unless you can call threats to kick our butts after

the game inspirational. Instead he makes quick adjust-
ments in the offense and defense.

This time he makes a major adjustment in the offense.

"Dillon, Cameron. Over here."

Dillon and I walk over to Coach. He's standing with one
leg hiked up on the bench, clipboard resting on his knee.

"Dillon," he says, "I'm putting Cameron in."

Dillon swallows hard and nods his head.

Coach looks at me. "Okay, Cal?"

"Okay."

We go over a few things together. He tells me that one
of his assistant coaches will be calling the plays.

"Listen to him now. You play it as he calls it," Coach
says. "Nothing fancy."

"Right," I say.

Halftime is over. We take off for the field. The Geekman
is there at my side.

"Way to go, buddy," he shouts into my ear.

"You yell for me," I tell him. "You hear?"

And then I pick up the pace and leave Geke behind,
waving me on.

The thing is, when I walk onto the field, I feel calm.
Pumped but calm. For the first time all year I feel like I've
got it together.

We don't do anything flashy, but little by little we start
chipping away at their score. Just as important, we don't
let them get any more.

It's sort of a weird thing, watching a good team come
unglued. They start making stupid little mistakes. They
shoot offsides. They hold. They start turning the ball over.
That's what happened to this team. Whereas in the first
half they could do nothing wrong, in the second half they
can do nothing right.

With two minutes left, the score is tied. We have the ball
on our own twenty. The trick is to hang on to the ball for
as long as we can and then score right before the game

ends. Coach sends in a series of running plays from the bench, designed to gain short yardage and eat up the clock.

Finally, with less than a minute left, we have twenty yards to go. Coach sends Sean in with another running play.

I can't believe it. For one thing, time is running out. We need to score and score quick. For another, the other team is catching on. You run an end around three times in a row and they get suspicious, you know what I mean?

So I do something. I call my own play and send all the receivers out.

This does take the other team by surprise, although most of their defenders manage to key on most of my receivers right away. Except for one. Sean is standing all alone in the end zone. I avoid a few rushing linemen, roll out, and pass. The ball hits Sean in the numbers and he hangs on.

The ref's arms shoot straight up in the air.

"Touchdown!"

The crowd erupts. Everybody is jumping all over Sean and me. He races toward me and gives me a high five. Then he throws his arms around me. He's crying.

As we watch the PAT attempt, Coach comes over to me.

"I told you no fancy stuff," he says.

"I know."

"Fortunately for your rear," Coach says evenly, "that wasn't the least bit fancy. It was just good smart football."

"Thank you," I say. "Thank you, sir."

9

So now I'm a hero. A star. Most of all, I'm one of the guys again. As far as Sean is concerned, I'm one great human being. And I feel nothing short of terrific if you want to know the truth. I felt in control out there. I felt like I knew who I was and like I knew what I wanted to do. I didn't want to play football for Granddad or Coach or anyone. I wanted to play for me. For the first time in a long time, football was fun again. What a feeling!

The next day at school there's almost a party atmosphere. You'd think we won the state championship already, what with the way everyone is acting. I guess no one thought we'd do it, so the surprise just added to the delight, you might say.

During the lunch hour, a bunch of the guys from the team hang out in the commons area together. The commons is a big indoor open area in the middle of the school. It's where people hang around, where the guys check out the girls and vice versa. You can sort of tell people's social status at our school by where they hang out in the commons. The soshes, of course, have prime real estate—right by the huge plate glass windows. The brains hang out in the part of the commons closest to the front office. The drama and music people take the corners, where they can bounce lines off each other. And the D-wingers, of course, don't hang out in the commons at all. They prefer dark bathrooms and parking lots.

Anyway, as I was saying, guys from the team are hanging out in the commons, mostly being very loud and, at times, pretty funny. Bear, for instance, does his imitations of the different teachers. He's at his best, however, when he does Coach. He pulls down his belt and throws out his stomach about a mile. Then he chews his tongue and scratches his head. "All right, you guys," he says and everyone falls on the floor.

Everyone is feeling pretty good. A guy named Lloyd Hanks pulls up his T-shirt and shows us a face he's drawn with a pen around his navel. Then he ripples his stomach muscles so the face talks while Lloyd does a voice.

"Can you say championship? I knew you could," Lloyd's belly button says. Great stuff.

Then, disaster strikes. Wally Geke walks across the commons area.

"Hey," says Sean. "Hey, Geke."

The Geekman looks up. "Yeah?"

"Hey, Geke," Sean says. "Come help us celebrate, man."

I'll tell you right now this makes me a little nervous. I've never once seen Sean deliberately seek out the Geekman unless it was to stuff him into a garbage can.

The Geekman himself looks a little suspicious as he approaches.

"I'm here," he says, "so celebrate."

Sean walks over to Geke and puts an arm round him. The Geek barely clears Sean's armpit.

"I understand," says Sean, "that you're a man with a dream." Then he says to the crowd, "this here is the next Johnny Carson."

I go cold. The Geek makes a move to get away.

"Hey, wait a minute," says Sean, collaring the Geek. "I don't know about these guys, but I think that's pretty great."

Some of the guys nod and agree out loud. They're all trading looks and smiling. You can guess what comes next.

"So do a monologue for us," says Sean. "We want a monologue."

The Geek looks around. He doesn't know what to think.

I stare down at my feet so that the Geekman won't catch my eye.

"Well, goll-ll-ee, Sarge," he finally says, doing his imitation of Gomer Pyle, "I don't know."

He's standing in the middle of a circle of guys right now. They start egging him on.

"Come on, Geke."

"Let's hear you, man."

"We want a monologue, Geke."

"Well"—the Geekman is breathing hard—"okay."

Oh, Wally, I say inside myself, don't do it. Please don't do it!

I look up and I see the Geekman getting ready to perform. He looks baffled, but pleased. Can it be possible that he really doesn't understand what's happening here? That he doesn't realize Sean is turning him into the biggest fool that ever walked the halls of Scenic View High School?

This is terrible. It's my fault. And I can't do anything about it.

Geke starts to tell a string of really terrible jokes in that high grasshopper voice of his. Everyone is sort of standing around choking with silent laughter. A few guys whistle and say, "Awright, Geke!"

The Geekman finishes up his routine.

"Hey, Geke," Sean says, "that was real terrific!"

A few of the guys clap their hands. By now a few more kids have gathered around. They're all in on the Big Joke.

"How about another one?" someone shouts.

Geke has started to loosen up a bit. "Yeah, okay," he says.

He starts another monologue.

Have you ever had the experience of watching someone in your family speak in public? You know how your palms get all sweaty and you start to take short breaths when they begin a joke you know is going to bomb? Well, that's how I feel, only a million times worse. Because Wally isn't about to make a fool of himself. He's already succeeded—with the help of Sean and Co.

Halfway through his second routine the Geek catches my eye. Something in my face must tell him what's going on. He stops.

"Hey, what's the matter, Wally buddy?" says Sean.

For once in his life Geke doesn't say too much. In fact he doesn't say anything at all. He just looks at Sean. Then he looks at everybody else. Finally he pulls himself as straight as he can and says, "Excuse me."

He starts to plow through the group. When he passes by me, he whispers, "God damn you, Cal."

That night I call Geke's house. Nobody answers. Then I try Marti's house. Her dad picks up the phone.

"Is Marti there?" I ask.

Marti's dad pauses for a minute. "Well, Cal," he says finally, "I'm supposed to tell you that she's not home, but I've decided to take a moral stand here. I'm refusing to lie for my daughter. Just a minute, please, Cal."

After I wait forever, Marti gets on the phone.

"Hello." Her voice is pure ice.

"Hi, Marti. I was wondering if I could come over to see you tonight."

"I'd rather you didn't," she says.

"Look, I really need to talk."

Pause. "Okay."

And then she hangs up the phone.

Quite obviously Marti is very angry. I knew she would be. I knew somehow she'd find out about today and that she would react this way. I have to talk to her, though, to tell her I know I did a creepy thing. I mean it may not be enough, but at least knowing what you did is better than not knowing. Or caring.

Marti's dad opens the door. He has this strange smile on his face. I can't really explain it except to say that it's sad and sweet, which I realize is a terrible way to describe a man, but it strikes me that way.

"Hi, Cal," he says. "Marti's waiting for you downstairs."

I go downstairs. The lights are off, but a fire is burning in the fireplace. Marti's back is to me.

"Hi," I say.

She doesn't turn around. She doesn't say anything.

I take a deep breath and walk over to the fireplace hearth. I sit down and face Marti.

"Well," I say, not knowing where else to start, "I guess you heard about what happened today."

"Yeah. Wally told me. I saw him right after it happened. He was so upset he couldn't talk, but I made him tell me what the matter was." Marti looks at me and her eyes are cold. "How could I have been so wrong about you, Calvin Cameron?"

I can't explain how terrible I feel when Marti says this.

"Look, Marti," I say, sounding pretty desperate, "I am sorry about what happened today. Honest I am. I was wrong. I was wrong to tell those guys about Wally's stupid monologues. I was wrong to let them set him up like that. I was wrong. I was wrong. I was wrong."

"You're just like the rest of them, Calvin Cameron." Her face and voice haven't changed a bit. It's like she hasn't heard a single word I've said.

I can see her building a wall between us—just like the wall she's built between herself and her mother and everyone else who has hurt or disappointed her. I can see her blocking me out. Looking through me. Turning me into nothing. She's had a lot of practice in doing this. You bet she has.

This has a curious effect on me. I stop groveling. I stand up straight. And this is what I tell her. "You weren't the only one who was wrong. I was wrong about you, too. Do you have any idea how much I admired you for daring to be different? I thought you had more guts than anyone else I knew. But I was wrong about you because the real truth is that you're a coward."

The words flow. I can't help myself. "You're a coward. You're the most afraid person I ever met. You want to know the real reason why you don't run real races? Because you're afraid you'll fall flat on your face and make a total fool out of yourself. Want to know why you keep to yourself at school? Because you're afraid you'll lose the upper hand in a relationship. You may even be a little afraid that people won't like you once you let them inside. Want to know why you won't even read your mother's letters? Because you're afraid of finding out how much you miss her."

This gives me another idea. "In fact, you're afraid you'll find out how much you two are probably alike. Geez! Your mother obviously thinks fish don't need bicycles and women don't need men either. Just like you. Only you hold it against her because your dad just happens to be the man she doesn't need.

"The real truth is that you're afraid of looking inside, Marti, and finding out what's there. What I did today to Wally Geke stinks. No doubt about it. But at least I know how much it stinks. At least I'm not afraid to take a look at myself."

By now I'm shaking. It's time to leave before I do something really stupid. Like cry. I reach into my jacket and pull out a program about the state playoffs. "I brought this for Freddie," I say. I toss it and it lands in a heap at her feet. I turn and leave without saying good-bye.

And she doesn't say good-bye either.

10

It's almost Christmas. We get out of school for the holidays today. Miss Shumway looks like she's passed the point of no return. An extended vacation away from Scenic View High probably won't help much at this point.

So this is what has been happening in my life since the Big Talk with Martha. Or I guess I should say the Speech, since technically she never said anything back to me.

We didn't win the state championship, but I ended up starting in the rest of the playoff games and I did fine. Coach is pleased. Granddad is pleased. Everyone on the team is pleased. And I'm pleased too. I think I felt so much pressure from so many people during the season that I balked. Rebelled even. But when I realized again during the playoffs how much I like to play, suddenly it didn't matter what anyone else expected, and I started having fun again.

Also—and this is really amazing—I've started doing okay in school. For once in my life, teachers aren't telling my mother at parent-teacher conference that I have "a lot of potential." I've always considered that a polite way of telling a parent that her child is a screw-off, a goofball of major talent. I don't know exactly why I've become Mr. Wizard all of a sudden. All I know is that when I go home at night and open my books I don't have to think about anything except what's on the page. I can forget everything else. Which, as you can probably guess, appeals to me right now.

Sean is no longer on my case. He assumes everything is just swell between us, and this naturally pleases old Bear. So now they call me up all the time for movies, partying, whatever. Only I don't go so often anymore. I always have an excuse handy, mostly that I'm doing cleanup work at my dad's office after hours now that football season is over.

I'm not doing much of anything with anybody else either. I haven't called Jennifer in weeks. Joy came up to me in school the other day and said she needed to talk to me "in private."

"What's the matter?" she asked me.

"What do you mean what's the matter?"

She gave me one of her really earnest I-want-to-help-you looks. "I'm talking about you and Jennifer."

"Oh." I didn't know what more to say. Have you ever noticed how there are some girls who don't seem to feel the least bit embarrassed about jumping with both feet into your personal business? I mean it would be one thing to a have a heart-to-heart with Joy if I knew her pretty well. But I don't. Still, here she is asking me what I consider to be pretty personal, direct questions. It seems like girls have this ability to slide into a personal friendship where you tell the other person everything within five minutes of knowing each other. I'm not that way myself, I guess. I don't like to talk about my feelings.

"Jennifer is really upset that you don't call her anymore," said Joy the S.B. She had this piece of gum in her mouth, which she popped every now and then between her teeth. "I mean, not that she needs you to call her. She's got plenty of guys calling her. But she wonders why you aren't calling her." Joy stared at me very directly. There was pressure in her look.

This is how tough I am these days, however. I looked at Joy and said, "If Jennifer is upset, tell her to talk to me. Not her girlfriends."

Joy narrowed her dark eyes into little tiny black slits. She cracked her gum again, then left without saying a word. Frankly, I was very glad to be rid of her.

So I'm not seeing Jennifer. I am also for sure not seeing Marti. We haven't spoken since that lovely evening in her basement.

I have to say I miss her, though. I also miss her dad and Freddie and Boy. I miss sitting downstairs in front of a hot fire.

So the bottom line is that I've been feeling lonely, see. Me. Calvin Simpson Cameron. The man who people are saying will be the next senior class president of Scenic View High School. It's Christmastime and I can't think of a single person I can really call a friend.

The bell rings. It's time to go. Home for the holidays.

I go to my dad's office after school to haul around some boxes for him.

"Hi, Cal!" says Annemarie when I walk through the door. Annemarie is my dad's long-time receptionist. She's about sixty now, but you'd never know it. She has a nice figure for a lady her age. She jogs and eats weird things like bee pollen and shows dogs as a hobby. Sometimes my granddad takes her dancing with the Silver Seniors. I think she's great.

"Hi yourself," I tell her.

She asks about school and I ask about Clyde, her favorite cocker spaniel. Then she says, "I need some help with billing this afternoon, Cal. Can you help me after you move the stuff in the back room?"

"Sure," I say.

On the way to the back, I poke my head through the doorway of the room where Dad is working. He has a patient—an old man—propped back. The guy's taken off his shoes, and from the doorway I can see that he has holes in his socks. Like his big toe—all white and milky-looking like most old people's toes—is sticking straight out and everything.

A lot of dentists don't like to do old people, but my dad doesn't seem to mind. I mean I guess he doesn't mind because he has tons of elderly patients. I can imagine them all sitting in rest homes around the valley saying, "Oh yes, I just love that nice Dr. Cameron." Something like that.

I don't say anything to Dad, because he looks so busy, so intense, about cleaning this guy's teeth. This is really amazing to me, but as I watch my dad I realize he actually *likes* his work.

Anyway, after I haul the stuff around out back—mostly boxes of insurance forms and toothpaste samples and stuff like that—I go back to help Annemarie with the billing.

She explains to me. "These bills go in the regular white envelopes. These go in the second-notice yellow envelopes. And these go in the blue envelopes."

"To the people," I say, "who better pay up or else." Then I do a tough-guy routine. "Pay in full or I will send Guido to break all your fingers."

Annemarie laughs. Then she says, "I only wish your father had a Guido working for him."

"Yeah?" I say absentmindedly, stuffing a bill into a white envelope.

"Yeah. Your father is a soft touch. He'll let people go forever without paying. Sometimes he doesn't even charge. As if good deeds count for anything in a business." Annemarie sounds mildly put out. "Well, he seems to be doing all right for himself anyway," I tell her.

"That's what he says, too. I tell him he's a middle-aged fool intent on becoming an old fool."

She still sounds annoyed, but she also sounds—how should I say it?—like she's fond of my father at the same time.

"So what you're really saying, Annemarie, is that my father is really kind of a nice guy."

"Yeah. I guess. A linthead, maybe, but nice."

We get done early and there's nothing left to do. I see my dad in his office.

"I'm going to do a little Christmas shopping," I tell him. He's looking at X rays.

"Okay, Cal," he says without looking at me. "See you about five o'clock."

Do you ever make mental lists about the ways you'd change people if you could? Like you'd make your math teacher floss his teeth every morning or you'd get your mother to stop wearing the same sunglasses she's had for ten years? Well, if I could change my dad, I would among other things change his habit of hardly noticing me when I talk to him.

Outside it's starting to snow. It's not dark yet, but most of the stores have turned on their lights. There are wreaths and Christmas trees everywhere. In front of one of the stores stands a group of old-fashioned carolers. Another store has a man out front with a cart of roasting chestnuts. Downtown Provo looks exactly like a Christmas postcard. I mean it.

I mess around mostly, although I do buy my mom some cologne at Walgreen's—Nina Ricci, her favorite brand. I'm looking at the magazines there when old Mr. Payne wanders in, blinking and mumbling.

It's funny to watch the different ways people respond to a guy like Mr. Payne. The young guy at the fountain waves and says in a real loud voice, "Hi, Mr. Payne." The lady with the high stiff hair at the cash register looks down her nose through a pair of bifocals and frowns. The people sitting around on stools and looking at magazines take a quick look, then turn away. Me, I'm staring without realizing it. He sees me and starts a slow shuffle over, a cigarette dangling as always from the corner of his lower lip.

Mr. Payne shuffles his way over to where I'm standing. I thumb through my magazine.

"You!" he says, talking to me. I can hardly ignore him now.

"Hello, Mr. Payne," I say.

He squints at me through eyes as bright as bright blue glass, then says, "God is a Finn."

"Pardon me."

"God incarnate is living in a small town in northern Finland, preparing now to save us all from ourselves."

"Oh."

"Yes! It is true." Mr. Payne practically roars at me. "We are in communication." Mr. Payne closes his eyes and a half smile like a baby's slips onto his face. "And *I* will help Him."

I look at this man and I suddenly find myself wondering what he was like when he was a little boy and thinking about his mother and how she must be dead now. How would she feel about her son? Would she love him still? I hope she would.

"Come on, Mr. Payne," I find myself saying. "Let me go buy you a cup of coffee."

We go to the fountain, and I tell the fountain help to fix whatever he can for Mr. Payne for five dollars. Then I lay the bill on the counter.

"I gotta go, Mr. Payne. Merry Christmas."

He turns to me. "My master and I bless you." Then he makes a sign in the air with his finger.

I leave Walgreen's and step outside into a cold bath of air.

People like Mr. Payne make other people uncomfortable. People like Freddie and Wally Geke, for that matter, make other people uncomfortable. It's like we're afraid of them, afraid of how different or odd human beings can really be, afraid that underneath we may have more in common with Mr. Payne than we want to. So we do all sorts of things to show how superior we are. We treat them like they're not even real—ignore them, laugh at them, trick them into singing private songs.

I feel the tears on my cheeks—I can't stop them. And all around me the snow falls in heap after quiet heap.

11

January.

I really hate January. For one thing, the weather is the worst. The snow freezes on the ground and the valley gets socked in with tons of cold gray fog. And then, of course, there are no vacations in sight at school forever. In the fall you're always getting out for something—pep assemblies, afternoon football games, Utah Education Association meetings, Thanksgiving, Christmas, even the opening day of the Deer Hunt.

Then comes January and you're stuck.

Eugene drives me to school the first day back from Christmas holidays. He leaves for school tomorrow. Actually, I found myself doing quite a bit with old Eugene the G. over Christmas break. I think my mom must have taken him aside and told him to be nice to his poor little brother who never invites friends over anymore. Anyway, Eugene took me up to Salt Lake a few times. We went to a star show at the Hansen Planetarium, where he hangs out, and also to this really different bookstore called the Cosmic Airplane, where Eugene stocks up on science fiction. We ate a lot of Chinese. Typical Eugene stuff, but it was fun in a weird sort of way. I was just glad we didn't hook up with any of his friends who go to restaurants dressed as their favorite *Star Trek* characters. He has this one friend, for instance, who calls the waitresses "earthlings" and flips a communicator out of his back pocket before ordering a pizza. I cannot begin to tell you how much I hate that kind of stuff.

Eugene pulls up in front of the school. "Well, here you are," he says.

"Thanks." I start to get out.

"Hey, Calvin."

"Yeah?"

"Thank you again for the book." He's referring to the book I gave him for Christmas—a book full of *Dune* trivia.

"Sure," I say.

He waves, then pulls off. I watch him go, wishing like crazy that it wasn't January.

When I go to first-period English, I notice amost everyone has something new on. Also, everyone looks a little sleepy.

Right before the bell rings, Marti slips in. She's wearing a new sweatshirt that says

A WOMAN'S PLACE IS IN THE HOUSE—AND IN THE SENATE.

She doesn't look at me. No big surprise there.

The bell rings. Miss Shumway hasn't shown up.

Five minutes go by and we still don't have a teacher.

"Hey, everybody!" Sean shouts from the back of the classroom. "We did it! We drove her crazy!"

A few people giggle a little nervously. Then the door opens and Mr. Molini, the principal, walks in. Things quiet up in a big hurry.

Mr. Molini is the kind of guy that no one likes but that everyone respects. He's sort of shrimpy, actually, with a soft low voice that sounds like a whisper. But when he looks at you he glares. He doesn't care what people think much, he just does what he thinks is right for the school. This drives people like Sean's mother crazy, because she can't push him around the way she did the principal at our junior high school.

Mr. Molini opens a book.

"Turn to page forty-five of your text. Now."

The sound of books plopping open fills the room.

"There are three exercises here. Do them. Then turn them in."

It's parts-of-speech stuff. Boring. But no one says a word.

Mr. Molini stays in the room. Miss Shumway doesn't show up. The secretary comes in and hands Mr. Molini a note. Something is up.

With about five minutes left, Mr. Molini stands before the class. "Miss Shumway will not be back. We will have a replacement by the end of the week." He doesn't say anything more, but the look in his eyes tells us that, according to him, we're worse than vermin.

The secretary's voice comes over the loudspeaker. "A call for you, Principal Molini."

He answers. "I'll be there in a minute." He glares at us again. "You're dismissed when the bell rings." He shuts the book and leaves.

Nobody moves, nobody says anything at first. Then Sean says, "I told you so." He sounds like he's gloating.

Then someone says, "You make me sick." It's Marti.

The bell rings. Everyone gets up, files out of the room, Marti last of all. As she walks past my desk I see that her skin is splotched from anger.

"Marti," I say.

She ignores me. And I know that she wasn't just talking to Sean. She was talking to me, too.

It's funny the way rumors start. By the end of the day there are a million stories circulating about Miss Shumway. Somebody said they saw her at the shopping mall with circles under her eyes and dirty hair. When they said hello, Miss Shumway just stared straight ahead and didn't answer.

"It was spooky," the kid said. "Just like she was a zombie or something."

Somebody else said they'd seen her at a movie. Halfway through the movie she got up and walked out sobbing, even though it wasn't a sad show. And then there were people who said no one knew where Miss Shumway was, that she had just gotten on a Greyhound one night after Christmas and disappeared.

It gives people something to talk about, that's for sure. Some people are saying that if she wasn't tough enough to take it, she shouldn't have been a teacher in the first place. But most people are saying that it wasn't really her fault. They aren't saying whose, but I know what they're thinking.

So does Sean.

At lunchtime he is pretty annoyed.

"They should never have hired someone like that in the first place," he says, picking up his tray. "And would someone explain to me where that chick with the thunder thighs gets off?"

He means Marti, of course.

Sean looks at his tray and swears for the millionth time.

I have to say there are times when old Bear surprises me. Now is one of these times.

"We were all pretty hard on her, Sean." He doesn't look up when he says this, he just keeps playing with his chow mein. But he says it, and it shuts Sean up.

After working for a while at Dad's office, I decide to go to the public library. I have a report due Friday.

It's freezing outside. And gray too.

In front of the library is a phone booth. I stop. An idea occurs to me. I go inside the phone booth and rub my hands together.

It's only 5:30, but it's already getting dark.

I pull out the phonebook and look under "S." I drag my

finger down the column until I see what I am looking for. She lives on Center Street, only three blocks away. I shut the book and leave the booth. The next thing I know, I'm standing on Miss Shumway's doorstep, panting for air.

A middle-aged woman answers the door. She eyes me without inviting me in. "Yes?"

"Hi," I say. "My name is Cal Cameron. I'm one of Miss Shumway's students."

The woman's face goes totally blank. In a flat voice she says, "I'm sorry, my daughter is resting right now."

From inside I hear a voice. "It's okay, Mom. Let him in."

Miss Shumway's mother lets me in, looking at me like I have several unpleasant diseases.

"Have a seat. My daughter will be with you in a moment."

I sit down and look around.

It's a nice little apartment. Small but clean. There are framed movie posters all over the wall. In the window there are three or four African violets. There are a lot of books on the bookshelves with titles like *Increasing Student Self-Esteem*. In a large bentwood rocker sits a teddy bear dressed like Humphrey Bogart. The television is on. It looks like one of those shows made in England.

"Hello, Cal." Miss Shumway is standing in the doorway. She has on a baggy sweatsuit.

Her mother immediately rushes over to her.

"Sit down, dear," she says. Miss Shumway sits on the couch while her mother tucks an afghan around her legs.

I try not to stare. She looks horrible. She looks thin and tired, and—as weird as this sounds when describing a young person like Miss Shumway—she looks gray. As gray as January.

"We heard you weren't coming back." I talk in the plural, like I'm sitting there with a bunch of other guys.

She manages a small smile. "It looks that way right now."

I don't know what to say. "Oh."

"The doctor says I need a rest," she says. As soon as Miss Shumway says the word "doctor," her mother, who's perched like a hawk on the arm of the sofa to begin with, leans closer to her daughter.

I tap my fingers on the arms of my chair.

"Well, I can't stay very long," I say. "I just want to tell you . . ." What do I want to tell her? "I just wanted to say I think you can be a good teacher someday."

Boy. What a stupid thing to say. I make it sound like she's not a good teacher now, which is true, but there's no point in bringing that up.

But Miss Shumway just smiles. "You're a nice person, Cal. Thank you."

Her mother gets up from the arm of the sofa. "You better go now," she tells me.

"Yeah, well I need to go to the library." I get up. "We'll see you around, Miss Shumway."

"Maybe, Cal."

I go outside, shutting the door behind me. I take a deep breath. The air is so cold it hurts my lungs.

I start to run, very slowly, very rhythmically, down the street to the library on the corner of Center and First East. In my mind I start chanting a poem I memorized for a program in the third grade.

> Tiger! Tiger! burning bright
> In the forests of the night . . .

My feet hit the pavement in time with the syllables in my head. When I was little and I was scared, my mom would tell me just to say a poem or the words of a song and chase the bad thoughts away.

> What immortal hand or eye
> Could frame thy fearful symmetry?

Here I am, running down the street, chasing the bogeyman away.

12

Going to school early is a very strange experience. The halls look wider, longer, definitely cleaner. It's like going to a stadium or a shopping mall when no one else is there. The place feels deserted—you half expect to see a tumbleweed blow by.

I'm here early today because I'm working on a project for Miss Tanner's class. She said she would be in early today and that I could come in to use one of the microscopes.

I walk down the hall, close to the place where I know Marti has her locker. I don't see much of Marti anymore. First semester ended a week or so ago and our first-period English class was broken up. We all have different schedules. Occasionally I get a glimpse of her in the library or across the lunchroom.

As I pass her locker, I notice that there's a piece of notebook paper taped onto it. I stop and look at it. What I see makes me cold.

Scrawled in big black letters is the word DYKE.

It looks so ugly, so obscene—the way it's written, the word itself.

I grab the paper and pull it down. Then I crumple it up into a tiny wad and stuff it in my pocket so that no one else will see it.

Miss Tanner is in the lab ahead of me. She's sitting at her desk, grading the quizzes we took yesterday.

She raises her head when I walk through the door.

"Hello, Cal," she says. "Here, I've just graded your quiz. Take a look."

I walk to her desk and take the paper from her hand. A hundred. My hand is shaking.

Miss Tanner is staring at me. She doesn't say anything.

"Geez," I say, trying to manage a little laugh that sounds halfway normal. "I'm turning into my brother."

She's still looking at me hard. Then she says simply, "Very nice work, Cal."

I hand her back the paper. Then I get a microscope and some slides from the closet.

While I'm setting up, I hear a familiar voice.

"Hel-lo!"

It's Marti coming through the door. She isn't saying hi to me because she hasn't seen me yet. I think I'm the last person she would expect to see here anyway. I don't generally lurk around the lab at odd hours. Igor I am not.

She turns around.

When she sees me, her mouth literally flies open. "Oh! You!"

I have to laugh in spite of myself. If it's typical of Miss Tanner to give a quiz the first week of school, it's just as typical of Marti to say the very first thing that pops into her head.

To my surprise, she laughs, too. "Sorry, Cal. I'm just surprised to see you here at the crack of dawn."

"Gee tanks," I say, imitating Rocky Balboa. I'm wrong. I'm not turning into my brother. I'm turning into the Geekman.

"Marti's been coming early for the past few months now," Miss Tanner says. "The university has contracted out some work they need done, and Marti comes in before school every morning."

Marti crinkles up her nose. "Mounting chiggers."

"Mounting who?" And then I turn bright red.

Marti bursts into laughter. Her eyes crinkle. "Mounting

what, you mean. Mounting chiggers. Little teeny-weeny bugs. Putting them on slides."

Now I can't think of anything to say. "Oh."

"So," Miss Tanner says, with only your basic hint of a grin, "if you're interested in making some extra money, Cal, let me know. They have plenty of work they want done."

"Well, thanks, Miss Tanner, but I already have a job right now. I'm working for my dad after school."

She nods, then turns back to her paper.

Marti gets a box of stuff from the back of the room, then goes to work.

I ask her a few general questions about her new schedule, and she asks me. I feel the wad of paper rub against my leg through my pocket lining.

Then it gets silent and we both go to work. Except I'm not thinking about my project. I'm thinking about how glad I am that I made it to school before Marti so she didn't have to find what I found on her locker.

Then it hits me. Who's to say that this was a one-shot deal, that there aren't going to be any more notes.

I get the shakes right there.

Just before eight, Marti clears up her stuff.

"I'll see you later," she tells Miss Tanner. Then she turns to me and says in a voice that sounds almost shy, " 'Bye, Cal." She goes out the door.

The halls are getting noisy. You can hear lockers slam and kids yell at each other. I have Miss Tanner for first period, so I don't have to go. "You should start putting some of your things away, Cal," she says.

I'm thinking. Finally I say to Miss Tanner, "So I can get paid to do what Marti's doing?"

Miss Tanner nods.

"How much? Minimum wage?" Not that I really care, but it seems like the smartest thing to ask under the circumstances.

"It's piecework, Cal. You get paid per slide."

"Oh." I think a minute. "Is there plenty to do? I mean I wouldn't be cutting in on Marti's work or anything would I?"

"I told you there was work for you if you were interested."

"Hmm. Well, I guess I might be, now that I think about it." I sound like a very bad actor.

"That would be fine, Cal. Starting tomorrow?"

"Yeah." And I'll get here before Marti. Every single day.

When I tell my dad that I'll be going to school early from now on, he looks up from his dinner plate and blinks. "Why?"

"Oh," I say, "I'm going to be doing a little work for Miss Tanner." I hope this will satisfy him, that he won't ask me any questions about what kind of work.

"What kind of work?" he asks. Naturally.

"Miss Tanner's got some kind of deal with the university. They pay kids to mount slides for them."

I know it's coming. He's going to blow. He's going to say, "What, I don't pay you enough?" Something like that.

But old Dad surprises me.

"Really?" he asks. "I did something similar to that when I was going to college. I started out as a literature major, but I found out that I was really interested in the biological sciences." Then he plows back into his potatoes.

I'm speechless. My dad, a lit major? He may as well have told me he was a major league baseball player. Or an astronaut, for that matter.

Parents. You think you have them all figured out. Then they do something that surprises you. They turn human on you.

* * *

So I start going early to school every morning for the joy, the thrill, the ultimate bliss of mounting chiggers on slides.

Usually I walk, which is no great fun in this kind of weather, but sometimes my granddad picks me up. He's friends with the shop teacher, who lets him in the workshop before school to tool around for a while. My granddad doesn't have much to fill his days up with since he retired, I've realized, which is a major reason why he's such a pain in everyone's rear sometimes.

No matter how I get there, I always make it to school before Marti and I always—emphasize *always*—pass her locker.

There's a note every day except for Thursdays and Mondays. Three weeks now, and it's always the same pattern.

The notes themselves have started to change, though. They were all pretty simple at first, like the first one— variations on the word "lesbian." Someone, I figure, must have found themselves a pretty complete thesaurus.

But now the notes have turned into little messages—gay jokes mostly. Stupid and crude, like the jokes you tell each other in junior high during gym class.

I can't figure out who's doing it. Or when. Or why. The notes are done in big black block letters, so it could be anybody's handwriting. They just must want to bother Marti bad enough to get up early enough to beat me here.

This morning the note has taken a particularly nasty turn. It says, "Everyone knows what you and Miss Tanner do first thing in the morning."

The note not only makes me sick to my stomach. It makes me angry. Angrier than I have been.

I remember one of the first conversations I ever had with Marti, the one where I hinted that Miss Tanner might be gay. I feel ashamed of myself.

I crumple the note and stuff it into my pocket. Like with the others I'll take it home and tear it up and either burn it in the fireplace or throw it away. I look at my watch, then I head for Miss Tanner's room. As always, she's there.

For half a minute, I very seriously consider telling her about what's been going on, especially now that her name is being mentioned. But I decide not to for a couple of reasons. First, while Miss Tanner is a person I respect and like, she isn't really warm, as you may have noticed. She certainly isn't like the high school counselor, Miss Rogers, who wants to go around and have heart-to-hearts with all the student body officers. And second, given the fact that I'd have a hard time talking to her about anything personal in the first place, it would be especially difficult to tell her that somebody thinks she and Marti are girlfriends. Get the picture?

Besides, what could she do? Geez. I feel so alone right now.

"Cal?" It's Miss Tanner. She's staring at me. I realize I'm just standing by the closet. I haven't even said hello yet.

"Oh." I shake my head like I'm trying to wake up still. "Sorry. Hi."

At that very moment, Marti breezes through the doorway. I practically jump out of my shoes. I get the willies just thinking about how close she came this time to finding the note on her locker.

"There's a lot of work this morning," Miss Tanner says and gives us both a look that says get busy. NOW.

Actually, Marti and I have been getting along pretty well since that first morning when we both started laughing together. Things aren't the same, though. We don't see each other otherwise, and I get the feeling that Marti's busy after school these days, although doing what I don't know. It's like she wants to keep it a secret. I think it must be a guy. Some new boyfriend she found over Christmas vacation. It could be one of her dad's art students—one of those tall thin types with sensitive eyes who wears a turtleneck and likes jazz. Well, that's okay, I guess. If that's what she wants.

So we both get busy and don't say much. When the bell rings, Marti says, "Freddie says hi, Cal. Dad too."

"Oh," I say, "yeah. Well tell them hi too."

"I'll do that." Then she laughs, a little shy it seems to me. "I'll see you later, Cal."

"Right," I say.

Then she leaves.

As I watch her go I tell her quietly, please, please don't let yourself get hurt.

There's an old saying—maybe you've heard it—that the mechanic's car is always in the worst shape. It's like he's so busy taking care of everybody else's cars that he doesn't have time left for his own. Well, I don't know if it's always true, but it certainly is in my grandfather's case. It's a family joke that if you need to be anyplace important like your mother's funeral or something, you can count on Granddad's truck, the Ole Grey Goose, to break down on your way there.

So why am I so surprised to be freezing to death with my granddad on the side of the road here this morning?

We're about two miles from the school. When the pickup chugged to a stop, my first thought was that I had to get to school no matter what. I had to get there before Marti did.

But then I reconsidered. It would be nothing short of criminal for me at the height of my youth to run off and leave an old man with a broken-down truck. So I stick around trying to help, listening to Granddad swear and call me a gnat with no brains.

He finally manages to fix the truck. We get in and bump

along to the school. I fly out of the cab and into the building. Marti's locker is in main hall. I turn the corner, and as
you probably guessed, I see her standing there holding a
piece of paper in her hand.

"Marti!"

I yell down the hallway.

Her head bobs up quick as a rabbit's.

"Marti," I say, only not so loud this time because I've
nearly caught up with her.

She hands me the paper. It says, "What do you call a girl
who loves other girls?"

"Oh, Marti," I say.

She looks at me through narrow eyes. "There've been
others, haven't there?" she asks in a tiny voice, almost a
whisper.

I nod, miserable.

"I've been coming to school early and taking them off
your locker."

She looks down at the floor. Then she looks back up and
I see tears in her eyes.

"Oh, Cal," she says.

I tell Miss Tanner that Marti and I won't be working
this morning. She raises a thick eyebrow but says okay.
Then I meet Marti at the library. We sit in the corner
behind the physical-science stacks.

Marti isn't crying anymore, but her cheeks are puffy.
"Were all the notes"—she pauses for a second— "like this
one?"

I nod. "More or less. Same subject, if that's what you
mean."

"That's what I mean." She lets out a deep sad sigh. It
occurs to me that I've heard Marti sound mad, happy, and
amused. But I've never heard her sound sad before.

We sit there together for a while without saying anything. Then she says, "Who hates me bad enough to do this? Nobody knows me well enough to hate me."

"Hmm," I say. "It seems to me lots of people hate each other because they don't know enough about each other." I'm thinking about my current events class—Arabs and Israelis, Catholics and Protestants. Geez. I'm turning into such a thoughtful sort these days. A real intellectual.

"Hmm." Marti thinks about what I've said for a while.

Kids are starting to pile into the library now, including this one bunch who wear old army jackets. I've seen them in here before. They play some sort of game about wizards and stuff every morning before school. It's the sort of thing Eugene would do. You wonder how they got interested in that stuff. You wonder why they are the way they are and you are the way you are.

Marti pulls her sweater around her a little tighter.

"You know what's really weird?" she says.

"What?"

"Something like this makes you paranoid. I look around here and I see all these people and I think, 'Did you do this? Do you hate me?' "

She doesn't say any more. But she does slide her hand across the table and take mine.

So this is what we do. We start treating the notes like they're a great big joke.

"So what did they say today?" I'll say when she comes into the room.

"See for yourself." She'll slip me the note. "You'll notice that they misspelled *orgy*."

"Because it's not on the junior spelling list."

Marti will pull a face at me, then get busy. She's being really cool about the whole thing. But I know how much the notes bother her.

I've noticed something about the notes. Marti's right.

Although I wouldn't have noticed it on my own, a lot of the words are spelled wrong.

Something starts to click in my brain, but I can't hold on to it. Do you ever feel that way? Like you're on the verge of thinking of something, of figuring something out, but then it won't come? It drives me crazy when that happens. Totally nuts. When I was a little boy, Dad told Eugene and me that if we ever caught a pigeon in the park, we could take it home with us. So we'd sneak up behind the pigeons and make a grab for them. Of course they always flew away at the last second, even when you thought for sure you had them. That's how this idea feels. I can almost make a connection. But not quite.

13

I once saw a painting of a baseball player connecting his bat with a baseball. The name of the picture was "Moment of Perfect Joy." I don't know if the picture was good art, but I liked it because it captured perfectly how I feel about baseball.

If you want to attract attention as an athlete around here you play football or basketball. You don't play baseball. Nobody—except Wally Geke and my granddad—comes to the games, which are in the afternoons during the spring before school gets out. You play baseball at Scenic View High because you love it. And I do. I have ever since I was eight years old and started playing in the city's Little League program.

I don't know what it is about baseball, but when you stand out there in the field with the green and the sun, time sort of stands still.

I say all this because baseball practice starts today. And since the weather is good—we had an early thaw this year—we're playing out on the field.

The Geekman is the manager again. I've never known anyone who knows as much about the history of the game and players as the Geek. He's like a walking baseball card collection—he knows stuff like who stole the most bases in the 1968 World Series and career batting averages for practically every human being who ever played the game.

The Geekman, in fact, is getting equipment together this very minute.

"Hey, Wally," I say.

"Hey, Gube," he says. The Geekman and I have sort of drifted back together. He figures I owe him now, so this means I get to take all sorts of his abuse.

I look at him, all short and hunched over with his bad leg, and I think how strange it would be to know so much about a game you can't even play.

We go outside, where the guys start tossing baseballs around. It feels good to be moving.

From a distance I can see the football field. The men's and women's track teams are there working out. Their first meet is Saturday morning. I may go watch.

"Hey, Cameron." It's Sean. "This one's for you."

He throws the ball hard. I snag it easy. No problem.

"Where've you been hanging out lately, pal?" he says, moving closer.

"The library," I say.

"The library?"

I throw the ball back, then flutter my eyelids and look heavenward. "Oh, yes. I discovered the pleasures of the mind," I coo in a real high voice.

Sean laughs as he grabs the throw. "You," he says, "are getting weird."

We play catch for a while and I laugh at all Sean's jokes. I had almost forgotten that he can be a very funny guy at times.

I keep glancing in the direction of the track. All the guys do, most of them without even thinking about it. You always look when there are girls around. Most of them are in sweats, so the view isn't that great. Besides, they're a long ways away.

I do see one girl running around the track, though. I notice her because from here at least she looks a little like Marti. But I know that Marti would rather have her wisdom teeth pulled out without anesthesia than be on a team.

Practice goes pretty well in spite of Coach Lewis. Coach Lewis, I must explain, is one of the world's true morons. He's the sophomore health teacher here. I'll never forget one day last year when he said you could get syphilis from the air. The next day Sean came with a bag of his dad's surgical masks and passed them out. It was a great joke. It would have been even better if Coach Lewis had noticed.

Today he's put on John Philip Sousa records over the loudspeaker to "inspire" us. Like I say, the man lives in another dimension.

After practice I notice Sean sitting in the locker room. His looseleaf is open on his lap. He's writing something. A couple of guys are standing around him, and—this is the only word I can think of—they're giggling—just like Joy and Jennifer.

Sean hears me and looks up with a start.

"Oh," he says smiling, "it's just you."

"Doing homework? In the locker room? Now who's the genius?"

Sean laughs and so do the others. "We've been studying Greek mythology lately."

Greek mythology? I think. What's going on here?

"Did you know," Sean goes on, "that there was an island called Lesbos? Only women lived there."

The guys start giggling again.

I feel a slow burn move up my face.

It's been Sean all along. Sean has been writing the notes and leaving them on Marti's locker, first after basketball practice, now after baseball practice.

It makes sense. For one thing, Sean can't spell. He once spelled *unit* like *you-net*. You get the picture. For another, Sean is just mean enough to do something like this.

I should have seen it earlier but I didn't. I guess a part of me still didn't want to do what I'm about to do now.

"You've been leaving those notes on Marti's locker, haven't you?" I say.

Sean shrugs. "Yeah, that's right. So?" Then he looks up at me. "Hey, how did you know, anyway?"

"Because I've seen them. Every morning. And I've taken them down. Every morning."

The smirk slides right off of old Sean's face. He narrows his eyes. For a minute I think he's going to paw the ground and charge.

"You've been taking the notes down?"

"That's right," I say.

"Why?"

"Because even if the notes were true, they were totally low-class. Completely bush-league, Young. For another, they were wrong. Marti isn't queer. I know that much from personal experience."

For a split second Sean looks as if you could blow on his face and he would fall over backward. But only for a split second. Off and on the field, Sean always lands on his feet.

"Hey, this is great," he explodes with a laugh. "Cameron here is in love with a girl who's in love with a girl."

The other guys look at me, and then they laugh too—a little.

I feel like hitting Sean right in his fat arrogant face. But I don't. Instead I throw my gym bag over my shoulder.

"You're a real funny son of a bitch, Sean, you know that?"

For a minute he looks like he's going to come after me, but he's too smart for that. As long as he can laugh at me and everyone else, as long as he can put the world down, he has the upper hand. I'll say this. You got to give the guy credit for his instincts. I turn around and leave.

Good-bye, I say, as I walk out the door. Good-bye, parties. Good-bye, senior class presidency. Good-bye, popularity.

Good-bye, Cal Cameron Creep.

* * *

I go to Marti's house right after that. I take a big chance and go without calling first.

Her dad opens the door.

"Cal!" He seems genuinely pleased to see me. "Come in."

Freddie comes barreling down the hallway and gives me a couple of high fives.

It's funny. I haven't been here since that day in November, but it feels like I've never been gone.

"Is Marti here?" I ask.

"Sure," he says. "Downstairs."

I start down. Freddie starts after me, but his dad collars him. "Stay here, Freddie," he whispers.

Marti is sitting on the floor in front of the couch. Boy has his head in her lap. Marti's eyes are closed.

"Marti?" I say softly.

She starts, sees me, then laughs.

"Sorry. I must have fallen asleep. I've been so tired lately."

"Getting up at six in the morning to mount chiggers will do that to you."

"Mm," she says. "Among other things." She smiles again, and I get the feeling—again—that she's got a big secret. I feel a little sick inside and wonder what his name is.

"Will you go for a walk with me?"

"Honest, Cal, I don't think I could move right now. But a ride—yeah, I'd go for a ride."

And so we do. We put Boy in the back seat of the nerdmobile even though I know my dad is going to throw a fit about the dog hairs.

We drive around Provo for a while without saying much, just listening to the radio. Neither of us says much. An old Beatles song comes on.

"I know who has been putting the notes up," I say finally.

Marti doesn't answer, but I can see her back stiffen.

"It was Sean, naturally. I'm only surprised that I didn't think of it earlier."

"How did you find out?" she says.

I provide her with blow-by-blow coverage. She doesn't say anything. We keep driving. I notice that the orchards around Provo are beginning to bud. Spring already. Soon school will be out. I can't believe it.

"What are you doing Saturday?" Marti asks. Her question takes me a little by surprise. I don't know what I expected. Tears? Death threats directed Sean's way? Not this.

"Well, I don't know," I say. "Granddad wants me to take him to the track meet Saturday."

"Are you going to go?" she asks.

I shrug. "Maybe." Maybe, I think, unless you can make me a better offer.

But she doesn't. She just says, "Oh."

So I end up going to the track meet with Granddad. It's just a two-school meet—no big deal—but it's the first meet of the season, and I want to see what kind of shape everyone's in. Granddad, as you probably expected, likes track, too.

I wait for him on the front porch. My dad comes out to pick up the mail. He stands there with me for a minute, trying to make small talk.

Granddad pulls up and honks and I say good-bye. When I get into the van I see Dad still standing there all alone on the front porch. I know he's watching us. I feel—how can I say this—a little sorry for him.

"Maybe we ought to ask Dad if he wants to come with us," I say.

"Naw, laddie. Your father isna sportsman," says Granddad. And then he guns the engine and roars away without looking back.

It's another terrific-looking day. The sun is high and bright and the sky is blue. When we get to the track we see more people out than I expected. Good weather in early spring makes people around here want to get outside.

"Hey, Cal!" I hear someone shouting up to me in the bleacher.

It's Freddie. He's with his dad and Wally Geke. Marti isn't with them.

I wave.

"Mind if we sit with you?" Mr. Jeffs asks.

"Come on up," I yell.

I am really wondering where Marti is. With her name-less boyfriend? Then I have an idea—maybe she's seeing Danny, the kid with the kestrel. Maybe that's why she's gone on a Saturday morning.

Mr. Jeffs, Freddie, and the Geek join Granddad and me. Granddad sits glued to the same spot, arms folded, legs crossed. He won't slide over and give up his spot, so this means everyone has got to crawl over his knees. In case you haven't noticed, my granddad can be a little difficult at times.

"Nice day, isn't it?" Mr. Jeffs says to my granddad.

"Yeah," I answer for my granddad. Granddad doesn't feel obliged to answer people's questions if he doesn't want to.

Meanwhile, I have a question of my own. It has to do with Marti and where she is right now.

The call for the women's mile comes over the loud-speaker.

"Look, Daddy," screams Freddie. He points to the field below. It's Marti—all decked out in a Scenic View High School warmup suit.

"Surprised, Cal?" Mr. Jeffs asks.

"Yeah," I say, "I guess I am." Actually, totally blown away is more like it. Marti takes off.

Marti sheds her sweats and steps onto the track along with the other runners.

"Runners take your mark," comes the voice over the loudspeaker. Marti and the others stand poised in a pack. She keeps her head down, waiting for the sound of the gun. Good girl, I say. Good girl.

The gun fires. Marti takes off.

"Go, Marti!!" Mr. Jeffs is already on his feet screaming, and the first lap hasn't even been completed yet.

One girl from the other school is out in front. Marti is running with a pack behind her.

One lap down, three to go. I check my watch. So far, so good.

Marti's dad is still screaming. My granddad, of all people, is giving him looks of disgust.

Halfway through the race the pack has thinned out. Marti is running with two other girls. They all trail the leader. She looks good, though. Strong. Controlled. She doesn't look like she's about to fade. You never can tell, though, especially with a first race.

With one lap to go, Marti is running fourth. Soon it will be time to make a move—if she has anything left.

Freddie is screaming along with his dad. The Geekman is yelling too.

Marti starts to move up on the girl in front and catches her.

"All right!" shouts Geke.

She passes her and starts to close on the girl running number two.

By now Mr. Jeffs has come completely unglued. Marti kicks and beats number two. There's only one person between her and first crack at the finish tape.

Marti moves closer and closer. The tape is just a few feet

away. Closer and closer. That's right, Marti, keep at her. Make her feel your breath on her neck.

"Take it to her, Marti," screams Geke. "Pow, Alice, right in the kisser!"

The tape is inches away. Marti is almost there. But the girl has one last incredible burst and she breaks the tape first. Marti finishes right after. She slows to a jog after crossing the finish line, then bends over.

"Come on," says the Geek. "Let's go down."

We thread our way down through the bleachers. "Marti! Over here."

Marti sees us. Still gasping, she walks over to us.

"Oh, baby," says her dad, grabbing her. "You were terrific!"

Freddie hugs her, too.

The Geekman, of course, tells her what she did wrong and how she can improve.

The track coach comes over and shakes Marti's hand.

"A really good first race, Marti. Excellent."

She nods and smiles. "Thanks."

Then she looks at me.

"Way to go, Thighs," I say.

That evening I go to Marti's house. Her dad orders a pizza and we have a party. Freddie shows me Marti's silver medal about a million times.

Finally we're alone—except for Boy, who keeps rolling over on his back to get me to play with him.

"So that's why you were never around," I say.

"Mm."

"You know," I laugh, feeling pretty stupid that I'm going to say what comes next, "but I thought you had some guy you liked." I shrug.

Marti laughs. "No. No guy." Then she says, "Remember when you called me a coward?"

I start to explain. "I only said that because I was mad."

"I know, I know," says Marti, waving her hand. "But you were right. No one has ever understood that about me. Not Dad. Not even me." Marti laughs a little. "Especially not me. After you left that night I really hated you, Cal Cameron. I kept running the whole scene through my mind again and again—you standing there telling me I was afraid, me staring into the fire. And every time I thought about that night I got angrier and angrier—especially when I thought about the things you said about me —about me and my mother. I kept thinking of things I should have said back to you."

"I felt bad afterwards," I tell her. "I was pretty tough on you."

"That's what I thought, too. At the time anyway. But then one morning I woke up and finally said to myself, 'Okay Jeffs, just exactly why *are* you so angry?' And I realized it was because you were right." She grins a little. "Sort of."

I reach for her, put my arms around her, bring her close to my chest. Neither of us says anything for a long time.

"She really hurt me when she left," Marti says in a quiet little voice.

"I know she did," I tell her. "I know."

Marti slides her arms around my neck, and I kiss her. It just feels like the smart thing to do.

Epilogue

It's the last day of school. Marti and I are sitting on the lawn in front of Scenic View High. We're looking at my yearbook, but I get the feeling that Marti is thinking about something else. I ask her what's bothering her.

She picks a blade of grass and puts the end of it in her mouth.

"I'm moving, Cal. Dad, Freddie, and I—we're going back to California."

This is terrible news.

"It isn't totally unexpected," she goes on. "We both knew Dad was planning to stay at the university here for only a year."

"Yeah," I say while my stomach does a quick dive, "I guess that's right."

We both stay quiet for a minute. I'm thinking about next year—what it's going to be like without her. I'll be honest. I don't feel like the most popular guy at Scenic View High right now. I didn't even bother to run for a class office, although that had always been in my personal game plan.

Marti practically reads my mind. "You'll be okay next year," she says with a smile. "You really will. You're going to have a great year in football. You'll be a hero. You'll have lots of friends."

"I don't care about that," I say a little defensively.

"Yes, you do," says Marti, "and that's fine. You're the kind of guy who likes people and who wants people to like you. The important thing is that you're not willing to do anything to get a friend."

"Well," I say, "I hope that's true."

"I know it's true."

"And you?" I say. "What about you?"

"Well, I'll go back to my old school, where I'll probably surprise a few people by joining the track team. Then after hours I'll take care of Dad and Freddie."

Marti picks another blade of grass.

"I've even thought about—you know—getting in touch with my mom."

I stare in amazement. "Really?"

"I've considered it. I really have. But I don't think I can do it. Not yet, anyway. Maybe not ever." Marti pauses. "The truth is that she's a pretty awful woman. I don't care what you think." She pulls a face.

For some reason this makes me laugh right out loud. It sounds so Marti.

And suddenly I feel better. Much. Marti and I will manage to keep in touch. Maybe she'll come back here to college. Or maybe I'll head for California as soon as I graduate. Who knows?

Just then I see Wally Geke. He's got a pocketful of pens —a rainbow of colors, he says, to match a rainbow of moods. I know I'm asking for trouble, but who cares? "Hey, Geke," I yell.

The Geekman stops. When he sees me, he snorts.

"Hey, Geke," I say, "come here. I want you to sign my yearbook!"

He starts to finger all those pens in his pocket as he makes his way toward me.

I know—totally stupid of me. But what can I say?